Jessica

***Also by Linda Lael Miller
in Large Print:***

The Legacy
Daniel's Bride
Forever and the Night

Springwater Seasons
Rachel
Savannah
Miranda

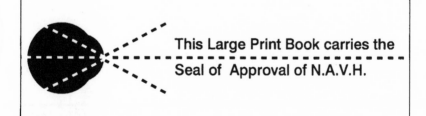

Linda Lael Miller

SPRINGWATER SEASONS
Book 4

Jessica

Thorndike Press • Thorndike, Maine

Published in 1999 by arrangement with Pocket Books, a division of Simon & Schuster, Inc.

Thorndike Large Print ® Americana Series.

The tree indicium is a trademark of Thorndike Press.

The text of this Large Print edition is unabridged. Other aspects of the book may vary from the original edition.

Set in 16 pt. Plantin by Juanita Macdonald.

Printed in the United States on permanent paper.

Library of Congress Cataloging-in-Publication Data

Miller, Linda Lael.
    Jessica / Linda Lael Miller.
       p. cm. — (Springwater seasons ; 4)
    ISBN 0-7862-2160-7 (lg. print : hc : alk. paper)
    1. Large type books. I. Title.
  II. Series : Miller, Linda Lael. Springwater seasons ; 4.
  [PS3563.I41373J47   1999]
   813'.54—dc21   99-33700

Jessica

Chapter

1

Winter, 1880

Behind her, Alma was weeping.

Plump, glistening flakes of snow swayed like languorous dancers past the bay windows set into the rear wall of the tiny parlor, but Jessica Barnes took no note of their feathery beauty. Her attention, indeed the whole of her being, was fixed upon the new grave in the churchyard just across the way. The place where her brother, Michael, a true and devoted friend through all twenty-three years of her life, lay buried. He had died precisely one week prior to her arrival yesterday in the remote Montana Territory town of Springwater.

How he had gone on about this place in his letters: the scenery was breathtaking, he'd written; the people had gathered him and Victoria in like family; there was so much sky that you could lie on your back in the deep, sweet grass, looking up, and lose yourself in all that blue. Not that he ever had time for such things, he'd been quick to stress, always working on the next issue of the paper the way he was.

Jessica swallowed a bitter sob. They had killed him, in her opinion — the work *and* the town. He'd always been a frail man, physically at least, and as far as she was concerned, the whole enterprise — buying that ancient press, traveling across prairies, deserts, and mountains in a wagon drawn by oxen — had been plain foolhardy. He should have stayed in Missouri, put aside his pride, and worked on their uncle's newspaper, as he'd been raised to do, instead of traveling way out here and exhausting himself. But no. Instead, he'd sold what little he had and turned his back on a respectable family business. He'd bought that huge, greasy, secondhand contrivance he called a press, dismantled it, and loaded it up — along with his frightened bride, a few sacks of dried beans, and a paltry assortment of supplies — for the journey west. Jessica recalled the day of their leaving with a clarity that stung even now, nearly six years later; seventeen and strong, she had begged to accompany Michael and Victoria on the trip west. Michael had refused her gently, saying it was far too dangerous a trip for a scrap of a girl like her — she was but a year younger than Victoria — and she'd realized that she would be in the way, an unwanted encumbrance.

So it was that she had, with her uncle's hearty approval, stayed and accepted a post as companion to an elderly but spry widow, Mrs. Frederick Covington, Sr. For two years she and Mrs. Covington had traveled on the European continent, and Jessica had enjoyed the experience and learned a great deal from her lively minded charge.

The dear old woman had passed away in her sleep on the journey back across the Atlantic, leaving Jessica a small, secret legacy and several pieces of jewelry, neither of which had been directly mentioned in her will. By that time Jessica's uncle had died as well, but there was no bequest this time — only a stack of demands from his impatient creditors.

She had sold everything — the newspaper, her uncle's modest house and personal belongings, even the clock from his mantelpiece — to settle his debts, and waited for Michael to send for her.

He didn't. The offer of a new position, in the household of Mrs. Covington's only son, Frederick II, and his wife, Sarah, had seemed a godsend. Appearances, however, were deceiving — unhappy in his marriage, Frederick soon began pursuing Jessica.

She had managed to avoid being alone with him for a very long time. Then one of the maids found the jewelry his mother had given Jessica on her deathbed, and, thinking Jessica had stolen it, turned it over to Mr. Covington. It was exactly the blackmail he needed. After that, he'd threatened her with ruin and scandal at best, prison at worst, if she continued to refuse him her bed.

She'd been prepared to plead with Michael and Victoria to take her in when, on the very day of Covington's ultimatum, her brother finally broached the subject himself in one of his more revealing letters. Things weren't going well, he'd written. Victoria was having a hard time with her pregnancy, and his debts were mounting. He suspected a certain lawyer, a Mr. Gage Calloway, of persuading the bank in Choteau to call in his loans. That was when she'd fled St. Louis for good and used part of the money Mrs. Covington had left her to travel west. What remained — and there was precious little — was secure in a Missouri bank.

Jessica brought her mind back to the present with a forceful tug. The injustice, the humiliation — all of it was too much to bear on top of losing Michael. She must think of it another time or, better yet, put it behind her forever.

Now, watching as the snow outlined her brother's plain wooden marker in an airy, lace-trimmed script, Jessica pressed the back of one hand to her mouth in yet another effort to contain her grief — and her fury. The world ground and clanked and clattered around her like the works of some enormous mechanism, and on the edges of her consciousness she was aware of Alma Stewart's soft voice singing a lullaby in the next room; the fretful whimpers of the two babies, left orphaned only weeks after their birth; the damnably steady, ponderous ticking of the mail-order clock on a rickety side table.

Wagons and buggies jostled by over rutted ground frozen solid beneath the snow, and both men and women called to each other in jovial, wintry voices. But beneath her feet, in the offices of the town's fledgling newspaper — the *Springwater Gazette* — the press was utterly still.

"Jessie?" Alma's gentle inquiry caused her to turn at last from considering Michael's final resting place. No one, save her brother, had ever called her Jessie, but she did not protest. Alma, too, was mourning, not only

11

for Michael, but for his wife — her niece — Victoria. Weakened by her own illness, Victoria had perished in childbirth, barely a month before Michael's fever, born of exhaustion and despair, took his life.

Jessica turned to face the deceptively delicate-looking woman who was just entering from one of the two nooks they called bedrooms. "Yes?"

Although she had a husband waiting for her on a ranch some forty miles away, Alma had come to Springwater when Victoria was due to have the babies, just to lend a hand. She was generous and capable and understandably anxious to get back home.

"He tried," Alma said staunchly. "He tried his best to hold on, Michael did. But when Victoria died, it was like something had been torn out of him. He worked himself blind after that, down there setting and resetting type and repairing that second-hand press all day and half the night. That was what finished him, Jessie. He just used himself up." Alma paused; her chin quivered and she dabbed at red-rimmed eyes with a wadded handkerchief. "You understand, don't you — I can't raise these babies? I'm an old woman, past the age for such things, and frankly it's all I can do most days to look after what's mine to tend. I've left a good

12

and patient man alone too long as it is."

Jessica had given little thought to children in general or to her infant nieces in particular, having been met with the news of both Victoria's and Michael's deaths directly after stepping off the stagecoach, though she had practically lived for word of them before fleeing St. Louis. Now, suddenly, she felt a fierce, almost primitive desire to protect them. They were so small, so fragile, so beautiful! Was this, then, what it felt like to be a mother, this swift and ferocious love?

They were a beacon of light, the twins were, in the otherwise impenetrable darkness of her grief, something to cherish and move toward. As dear as the Covington children — Susan and young Freddy — had been to her, and she had loved them with the whole of her heart, despite the contempt in which she held their father, this was a keener, deeper sort of caring. These babies were blood of her blood, bone of her bone, soul of her soul. They were *family*.

"It's all right, Alma," she said as tenderly as she could. She'd come west because Michael had summoned her at long last, because she'd had nowhere else to go, her reputation thoroughly spoiled, and she was set on taking hold and making a good life for herself and for the babies. "I'll provide for them."

Alma looked decidedly relieved as she groped for the back of a chair and then lowered herself shakily onto the frayed cushion of the seat. Jessica knew a moment of deep chagrin; yes, she had lost a beloved brother, and with shattering suddenness, but Alma had cherished Victoria, daughter of her long-dead and much idolized brother, Frank. Jessica knew all that from her correspondence with Michael. Alma and her husband had never had children of their own.

Settled at last, the older woman looked up at Jessica with eyes awash in tears. "You won't put those poor little darlings into a foundling home, will you?" she asked in a breathless rush. "Why, there are folks right around here who'd take them in. Good people. Gage Calloway told me just the other day —"

Gage Calloway. Now there was a name Jessica definitely remembered from her brother's letters. Mr. Calloway had wanted to be mayor of Springwater, and Michael had campaigned against him. He'd responded by using the power of his wealth to destroy her brother, however indirectly.

Jessica raised a slightly tremulous hand to call a halt to Alma's discourse. Under other circumstances she might have waxed indignant at the mere suggestion — consign *Michael's children* to an orphanage? — but she knew Alma's emotions were as brittle as her own, and therefore made a sturdy attempt to hold her annoyance in check. They were both doing the best they could under very trying conditions, and there was nothing to be gained by the exchange of harsh and hasty words.

Jessica straightened her shoulders and smoothed her black sateen skirts, as she generally did whenever she was challenged in any way. "You may rest assured that I will raise those children with as much care and devotion as I would if they were my own." She paused, then slid her teeth over her lower lip once, in a gesture of suppressed exasperation. Her voice, when she spoke, was almost plaintive. "How could you think for one moment that I would give them up? Those little girls are the only family I have now." Michael had no doubt told Alma how his and Jessica's parents had died in a carriage accident, leaving their two small children to be raised by a bachelor uncle who took little interest in the task.

Alma would not meet Jessica's gaze — not immediately, in any case — and even though she started at the sound of footsteps on the covered stairs leading to the crude board sidewalk out front, there was an air of profound relief about her, too. She had been spared making a reply and that was probably just as well. Michael, no doubt, had described his sister as a spinster, somewhat distant, with no knowledge or particular fondness for babies. The Covington children, being older, had needed an entirely different sort of care.

Indeed, she did wonder how she was ever going to adjust to Springwater, with its one store, one church, and scattered handful of houses. Without Michael, it had little or no appeal.

Patting her fair hair to make sure none of it had escaped its pins to tumble untidily down her neck, Jessica put her private reflections aside for the moment at least, crossed the room, and opened the door. The caller, a dark-haired man of imposing height, with eyes the color of malachite, had one fist raised, poised to knock. A chill wind rushed past him to nip at Jessica's very bones, and yet the sight of him caused a warm wrench, somewhere deep inside, leaving her with a sense of having turned some mysterious spiritual corner.

Always wary of strangers and equally determined to disguise that fact, Jessica lengthened her spine and did not even attempt a smile. The man's effect upon her was, she concluded, reason to be extra cautious.

"Good day," she said politely, if not warmly, lending the greeting the tone of a question. She might as well have told him "State your business and leave."

"Miss Barnes?" His teeth were as white as any she'd ever seen, and he smelled of fresh air and snow and the distant pine trees that covered the foothills.

She tried to look pleasant, if not exactly glad to see him. These were frontier people, and it was probably considered neighborly to pay a call on any new arrival. "Yes?" she said. She did not step back or invite the visitor inside. This was, after all, a household in mourning and, therefore, seclusion.

He removed his hat, a rather dapper affair with a round brim and a band of shimmering silver conchos, holding it in both hands. His hair was thick and had a silky gloss to it, Jessica noticed, and she was amazed at herself when she felt an instinctive desire to reach up and flick a lock of it back from his forehead with the ends of her fingers. Her reaction was curious indeed, and she would have been the last person who would presume to explain it.

"My name is Gage Calloway," the man

announced after clearing his throat once. Even that simple statement sounded eloquent coming from him, but of course it landed on her with all the weight of a derailed freight car. Here, then, was her brother's enemy. *Her* enemy, now that Michael was gone.

"I'm the mayor of Springwater." He paused, looking pained. "We're awfully sorry about your brother, Miss Barnes. The townsfolk, I mean. It must have been a real shock to step down from the stage and be told right off that a loved one had passed over. . . ."

Jessica's throat constricted at the memory; it was indeed fresh to the point of rawness, and her eyes stung. A sort of cold fury filled her, mingled with a deep sense of guilt because she knew she had instantly warmed to the man despite all he'd done. Had the visitor been practically anyone else, she would have invited him in, offered him tea, perhaps, and certainly a chair next to the fire. As it was, she simply could not make the necessary effort. "You will forgive us, Mr. Calloway —" she began, fully intending to send him on his way, but before she could complete the sentence, Alma interrupted.

"Why, Gage, it's dear of you to come

calling," the other woman said from the doorway of the tiny kitchen, in a voice Jessica would have sworn was fluttery. "Do come in out of the wind. I've put some coffee on to brew, and you look frozen straight through."

Gage Calloway met Jessica's unyielding gaze, albeit briefly, and nodded his acceptance of Alma's invitation. The smile he gave, reserved for Alma, was dazzling. "I wouldn't mind a few minutes by the fire," he allowed. "Looks like we're in for a pretty bad winter."

Jessica was left with no viable choice but to step aside, short of spreading both arms and barring his way. Judging by the size of Mr. Calloway, the effort would have been futile as well as ludicrous; he stood over six feet tall, and his shoulders very nearly brushed the door frame. "Yes," she said in a slightly clipped tone that was more defensive than scornful, "*do* come in."

A smile played at the corners of Calloway's fine, supple mouth as he entered. His eyes, though solemn with sympathy at the moment, were normally more given to mischief, calculation, and merriment, Jessica ascertained, via some as-yet-unrecognized sense.

"No one makes better coffee than you do,

Miss Alma," he said, though he was looking straight at Jessica all the while he spoke. "Just don't tell June-bug McCaffrey I said so. She's downright prideful about her cooking."

Alma made a sound that was part laugh, part twitter; maybe she didn't know that this man had been Michael's foe. In fact, it was obvious that she enjoyed Mr. Calloway's company, even in this time of sorrow. Probably a great many women would, Jessica thought pragmatically; she had to admit that he was a very attractive specimen, scoundrel or not. She, on the other hand, had good reason to dislike him.

His manner reminded her of her own nemesis, Frederick Covington. He'd been handsome, too. He'd had money and power, just as this man did. He'd also been a devil, and it was likely, given what Michael had said about Mr. Calloway in his editorials, that the two men were the same in that regard, as well.

When Alma went back into the kitchen, Jessica gestured stiffly toward one of the two chairs facing the inadequate brick fireplace. She had to make a home in Springwater for herself and for her nieces, and she needed the good will of the townspeople if the *Gazette* was to prosper. Therefore, she would be as civil to everyone as possible — including this man, however much it galled her.

"Sit down, Mr. Calloway," she urged, with a sort of wry resignation. He moved as gracefully as she imagined an Indian warrior might do, or a panther on the prowl. Inside, she seethed just to think of all the suffering he must have caused her poor brother.

He smiled as if they had every reason to be friends — it might have been more apt to say he grinned, for the expression was boyish — but hesitated. "After you," he said.

Jessica took the second chair, and her quiet rage was pushed aside by a fresh and sorely painful sense of sorrow. Surely Michael and Victoria had sat together on that very hearth many times, planning their happy life in Springwater. They'd dreamed of expanding the weekly newspaper to a daily, of building a spacious home and filling it with children. In more than one letter, Michael had referred to Springwater as "idyllic," though from what Jessica had seen so far, it was merely a small conglomeration of plain buildings huddled together in the midst of a fierce wilderness, like wild horses trying to find shelter from a high wind.

The babies had quieted at last, and Jessica almost regretted that, for a little fussing on their part would have given her a reason to excuse herself and leave the entertainment of this unexpected and most unwanted guest to Alma.

Once Jessica was seated, Calloway took a chair as well, and stared into the fire for a few long moments. She was just beginning to hope he did not intend to make conversation when he turned to her and said, "Your brother was a good man and an asset to the community. We all liked him, and Miss Victoria, too."

It was a bold-faced lie, of course. She'd seen Michael's editorials. This man could not have liked him.

Jessica felt tears threaten yet again — dear Lord, she was so weary of weeping, for she'd cried more in the past twenty-four hours than in all her life put together — and she did not like for Mr. Calloway, of all people, to be a witness to her weakness. She raised her chin. "Yes," she agreed. "Michael was a wonderful person, and Victoria was the heart of his life."

Alma reappeared just then, bearing a tray set with three cups and a steaming china coffeepot, and Mr. Calloway immediately got to his feet, managing to display proper deference by taking the burden from those small, blue-veined hands in one smooth motion. Jessica felt herself flush slightly — it was as though the floor had suddenly dissolved beneath her feet — and she looked away for a moment in order to recover her composure.

When she looked back, it was with narrowed eyes. Exhausted by grief and despair, coupled with the long and difficult journey out from Missouri, first by train and then by stagecoach, she felt downright peevish. She wanted to sleep for a month and cry for *another* month after that.

There was a small stir, in which Mr. Calloway found and brought over another chair, and Jessica, backbone rigid, observed the rites of hospitality out of the corner of one eye. Surely he would not stay long, she assured herself. He would take himself and the curious electricity that surrounded him *away.*

"I suppose you plan to sell the newspaper and go back home," said the mayor — that he'd triumphed in the election despite Michael's efforts to oppose him was one more reason not to like him — when what he probably regarded as a decent interval had passed. He looked down into his cup for a long moment, then raised those arresting eyes of his to lock with Jessica's. "It may be too soon to speak of such matters, ma'am — forgive me if I offend you — but I am prepared to make you a very generous offer on this place. One that should enable both you and Miss Alma to live comfortably for some time."

Jessica glanced quickly at Alma, who was watching the snow fall with a wistful expression. It probably would make sense to sell the *Gazette*, but now, in the face of an actual opportunity, she wanted to hold on to it more fiercely than ever before.

She raised her eyebrows slightly and stirred her coffee with a tinkling clatter of spoon against porcelain. "I should like," she announced, surprising even herself by the certainty in her voice, "to keep the *Gazette* for my nieces."

His expression sharpened, but it was only a moment before he had relaxed that spectacular face into a placid mask. Mr. Covington had possessed that same ability, that affinity for easy deceit. Both men were lawyers, members of a profession Jessica deemed only slightly above prostitution.

Calloway shifted in his chair, revealing only the mildest discomfort; no doubt even that was merely a pretense. Men like him spent their days and nights breaking as many commandments as possible.

He put his cup and saucer down and, with another glance at Alma, leaned forward a little way, his hands dangling between his knees, his fine round-brimmed hat resting on the floor beside his chair. Alma was still lost in her own thoughts, probably missing home and husband and thinking of household tasks that needed doing.

Jessica wondered what on earth she was going to do once Alma went back to the ranch. She'd never fed or diapered a baby in her life; indeed, until the twins were four or five, poor little things, she wouldn't have the first idea what to do with them. Only one thing was certain — she was fresh out of choices.

Calloway cleared his throat again and lowered his voice. "It has been mentioned that you, being an unmarried woman and all, might not wish to raise your brother's daughters on your own. I understand you've been serving as a governess for some time now, and that you travel a great deal in your work. Therefore —"

Jessica waited, content to watch him squirm a little and suspecting, with a sick feeling in the pit of her stomach, that she knew what he was going to say.

"I thought you might be willing to consider a formal adoption. My clients are able to offer your nieces a fine home —"

"Your clients?" She gave the words an edge. One of the babies began to cry and Alma rose, with a sigh, and toddled away to attend to the child. "Why, Mr. Calloway, you gave me the impression this was a condolence call. I suppose next you're going to tell me that Michael appointed you the executor of his will."

Jessica had been guessing, where the will was concerned, but it was plain from Mr. Calloway's expression that she'd struck her mark. The realization that Michael hadn't trusted her to serve in that capacity — indeed, that he had put more faith in his worst enemy — was devastating, but she managed to keep up her facade.

Calloway, meanwhile, had the decency to redden a little along the base of his jaw, but there was a glint of determination in his eyes, too. "Dr. and Mrs. Parrish are good people, Miss Barnes. Upstanding citizens, well-regarded by everyone in town. They have a four-year-old daughter of their own, but Savannah — Mrs. Parrish — well, they'd like more children."

A charged silence filled the room, punctuated only by the popping and shifting of the pine logs burning in the grate. The pleasant scents of wood smoke and stout coffee filled the room, and beyond the windows the snow, so quiet and so white, seemed sadly, poignantly magical.

When she could trust herself to speak in a moderate fashion, Jessica made her reply. "I'm sure your clients are very nice people," she said in tones measured out as carefully as a length of exceedingly fine cloth. "However, I have no intention of surrendering my brother's children — my only living blood relations — to anyone, however worthy they might be. If you have completed your business, sir . . ."

A muscle tightened in Mr. Calloway's closely shaven cheek, but he was a lawyer, after all, and he smoothed his features before Jessica could even be sure that he was irritated. "I'm sorry," he said, glancing in the direction Alma had taken when she left the room. "I was given to understand —"

Only then did it occur to Jessica, in her grief-addled state, that it had not been Alma alone who had suggested this arrangement, but Michael, too. Perhaps, even on his deathbed, he had been reluctant to leave the raising of his daughters to her. That stung even more than the fact that he'd appointed a virtual stranger to see that his last wishes were carried out.

She was filled with an inestimable and echoing sadness.

Still, she decided, after a few moments of inward reeling, she must make an effort to be charitable. It *was* possible that Mr. Calloway meant well, though not very likely. "I'm sure," she said, in what was almost certainly too abrupt a manner, "that you are only trying to help." She took a thoughtful sip of her coffee, which had grown cold, and her next words were meant to come as a shock. "I'm planning to run the newspaper myself," she said. "Provided that Michael left it to me, of course." She felt safe in assuming *that*, at least, since Mr. Calloway wouldn't have offered to buy the business from her if she hadn't been the rightful owner.

He looked truly startled, and did not even bother to comment on her statement, yea or nay. "You're not returning to St. Louis?" he asked. She couldn't rightly tell whether he was pleased or disappointed by this news, but he was definitely astounded. In all likelihood, she concluded, he did not care one way or the other *what* she did — why should he? — as long as he got what he wanted. "Your brother told me —"

"I don't care what my brother told you," Jessica lied, a bit pettishly. She wanted very much to know, but she was also weary to the innermost wellsprings of her soul, too weary to pursue the matter further. "I'm staying right here. In Springwater."

She had enjoyed her work in St. Louis before the trouble with Mr. Covington, not only because it paid unusually well, but because she was deeply fond of her two charges. In truth, however, the children were growing up fast and would soon go away to their respective boarding schools — Susan's in Switzerland, Freddy's in England — where, of course, they would not need a governess. She would have had to leave them soon anyway.

Besides, she had always wanted children of her own, and now she had them, even if they were her nieces and not her daughters. "This Dr. Parrish you referred to," she began cautiously, holding all her emotions at bay until she could sort them out, one by one, in the privacy of her own mind. "Did he look after my brother? At — at the end, I mean?"

"Yes, ma'am," Calloway said. He looked a mite grim, and had retrieved his hat from the floor to turn it slowly, round and round, between his fingers. "It isn't possible to find better medical care than you'd get right here in Springwater. Pres did everything he could to keep Michael alive, but he was real sick. The fever took him down fast."

Jessica closed her eyes against the image of Michael breathing his last, slipping away forever, but it was imprinted on her mind and she could not escape the force of it. She would gladly have died in his place but, alas, she had not been given a choice in the matter.

"I should like to speak with the doctor," she said, when she was fairly sure she would not break down and sob as she had done the whole night through. "There are questions I want to ask. About Michael's passing. And — of course — about Victoria's, too. I trust this Dr. Parrish attended her as well?"

The mayor of Springwater narrowed his eyes again, as if he were on the alert for a slur directed at the town doctor, who was obviously his friend. "Like I said, you won't find a better man anywhere than Pres is."

It was then that Alma returned. "I declare," she fretted, "that those two defense-less little darlings know they have" — she paused, perhaps for the sake of drama — "neither father nor mother to look after them." By then, Jessica was looking at the visitor, and not at Alma.

"They have me," she said pointedly. Then she rose from her chair, all dignity and bravado. She wasn't such a bargain, she reckoned, but she was a blood relation, and she loved those babies with all the scattered pieces of her heart. "We mustn't keep you, Mr. Calloway," she said. "You surely have a great many things to do."

Because Jessica stood, Mr. Calloway was, of course, forced to stand as well. She found she could not draw an accurate measure of his response merely by looking at his face, and that nettled her. He was a lawyer, she reminded herself, and that meant he had probably cultivated wily ways.

"If there's anything you need," Mr. Calloway said, and though he glanced at Jessica it did seem that his polite words were directed more toward Alma, "you just let me know. The people of Springwater look after their own."

Once again Alma was almost blushing, and Jessica glimpsed in her the pretty and charming girl she had once been, long ago. It was Alma, in fact, who saw Mr. Calloway most graciously to the door.

His departure was audible; his boot heels made a firm, even distinctive sound on the outside stairs.

When Alma turned back to face Jessica, her color was still high, and her eyes were snapping with uncharacteristic fury. "Whatever possessed you to be so rude to such a fine man as Gage Calloway?" she demanded, with such spirit that Jessica was quite taken aback.

She ignored the question, having no good response to make, and returned to her post at the set of windows overlooking the main street.

As she watched Mr. Calloway stalk across the snowy street, his strides long and angry, she smiled. What a good thing it was, she thought, that she did not have to explain her reactions to this disturbing man, for she did not begin to understand them herself.

Clouds were moving in from the west, heavy with still more snow, and the light was fading. Quickly Jessica hurried in to fetch her warm cloak.

"You're going out?" Alma asked, clearly surprised.

"I'll be back shortly," Jessica promised, and made for the door. The wooden stairway was steep and slick, exposed as it was, and she was careful making her way down. If she fell and hurt herself, she and the babies would starve.

Looking neither to the right nor the left, lest someone catch her eye and expect to converse, Jessica rounded the side of the humble newspaper building and made for the churchyard across the way.

She had some trouble with the gate, for the metal latch had frozen in place, but soon, by sheer force of will, she had wrestled it open. The snow, ever-deepening, was heavy, and she had to push hard before she could enter.

She raised her gaze briefly to look at the church itself. A small, trim structure, painted white, it boasted its own bell tower and mullioned windows. The double doors were closed fast against the cold — not that Jessica had any desire whatsoever to set foot inside. She and God were civil to each other, but that was the extent of the matter. Michael's death had only served to widen the gulf.

Holding her cloak more tightly around her, Jessica began slogging laboriously toward the small graveyard on the left side of the building. It was guarded by towering maple trees that were bare of leaves but lined with a fine tracery of frost and snow.

Her knees were wet by the time she gained the place where Michael had been buried. The snow was shallower there, hardly covering the still-raw earth of the grave. The wooden marker looked even more forlorn up close than it had from the apartment windows.

She blinked back stinging tears and breathed slowly and deeply. She was torn between kicking at the mound in pure outrage, and throwing herself down upon it in a fit of sobbing. Neither option was acceptable.

"I'm here," she said, and sniffled. Her nose was turning red — she could feel it — and her eyes were puffy. Her whole face felt swollen, in fact. "I'm here, Michael, and I'll look after the babies and the newspaper, I promise. Somehow, we'll all get by."

There was no reply, naturally, only more snow drifting down from the charcoal sky, and a wind that prickled even through her clothes. Jessica was seized by such a sense of loneliness that she might have been the only person in the universe, lost and wandering.

"You can depend on me," she vowed, in a whisper. Then she touched the cross once, where Michael's name was carved, before turning to make her way back to the gate.

Chapter

2

"Give the girl some time," June-bug McCaffrey counseled as she set the station house table for one of her legendary "plain" suppers. Her blue eyes gleamed with what struck Gage as tender amusement. "She's new in town, and she's just lost a close relation, into the bargain. 'Sides, those babies are her own kin, and it's a natural thing for her to want to raise them up herself. Poor little things. Why, I do believe I would think less of her if she'd turned her back on her own brother's children."

A bachelor used to being on his own, Gage was a competent cook, but he preferred June-bug's meals to his own concoctions and enjoyed passing an evening before the McCaffreys' fire, swapping tall tales with old Jacob. Especially a cold, snowy evening like this one. The big white house around the corner was as lonely as a tomb, and not much warmer, for all its fancy furnishings.

He'd been a fool to go to all that trouble and expense. For one thing, it reminded him too much of the place he'd grown up in, an echoing San Francisco mansion that was either empty or full of shouting and strife, but never peaceful and certainly never warm, the way the Springwater station was. He'd left California after one last shouting match with his tyrannical old grandfather, and he was never going back — not that he'd been asked. He'd ended up in Springwater purely by accident, liked the place, and stayed.

He thrust out a sigh. "I know you're right," he said to June-bug, recalling her assertion that it was only right for Jessica Barnes to raise her own nieces, "but Pres and Savannah are going to be disappointed that they can't adopt those little girls."

"Pooh," June-bug scoffed, with a wave of one competent hand. That was about as close as she ever got to swearing, at least in Gage's hearing. She and Jacob had been running the Springwater stagecoach station for a long while before the town grew up around it, and both of them were clear thinkers who generally spoke their minds. "Savannah and Pres have little Beatrice, and they know they're blessed. Why, the Lord may yet see fit to send them a whole passel of kids anyways. They're still young."

Jacob, a powerfully built man with a head full of dark hair, only lightly threaded with silver, had been holding his peace throughout the conversation, though he had a way of listening that made it seem like he was taking the sense of the words in through his very pores. Seated by the fire, he seemed intent on his whittling, but June-bug's remark inspired him to look up. The wooden horse he was carving looked minuscule in his big, callused hands. "I reckon Miss Barnes must have chosen not to sell you the newspaper," he said. "Seems to me, that's what's got you so riled, most likely."

Gage thrust a hand through his hair, which was still damp from walking hatless through the snow. "She took a dislike to me right off," he confessed, and wondered why it bothered him so much. Miss Jessica Barnes was a skinny little bluestocking with a snippy disposition, and her opinion oughtn't to matter the way it did. "She doesn't want to run a newspaper — probably doesn't have the first idea how to go about such a thing. No sir, I'd bet my best shirt that Miss Barnes had no plans to get into the newspaper business until she found out I wanted it. *Then* she got downright contrary."

June-bug gave a sigh of mock impatience. It had been a hard day and, frankly, the delicious scent of the elk stew she'd made for supper was about all that kept Gage from heading for the Brimstone Saloon to make a meal of hard-boiled eggs and beer. There were nights, and this was one of them, when he just couldn't face going back to that house by himself, that house he had so foolishly built for a bride who chose, in the end, to remain in San Francisco and marry his half-brother, Luke.

"Horsefeathers," June-bug said, jolting him out of his sorry reverie. "Michael fully expected his sister to help him put out the *Gazette*. He told me himself that he'd asked her to stay on permanent. He hoped she might even marry up with somebody from around here."

Jacob's dark eyes seemed to sparkle, but that might have been a trick of the lantern light. "She's a fetching little thing, Miss Jessica Barnes," he allowed. For Jacob, the most taciturn of men, this was unbridled, raving praise.

June-bug put her hands on her hips and tilted her head to one side. For all her sixty-odd years, she looked as coquettish in that moment as any dewy young maiden flirting by the garden gate. "Why, Jacob McCaffrey," she accused, half laughing, "I do believe you are *smitten!*"

He laughed, a sound like two great armies waging war in the distance, all but shaking the ground and rattling the windows. "I am smitten," he admitted. "Indeed, I am. With my bride of many years." He crossed the room, took June-bug's hand, and bent his head to kiss it. "That would be you, Mrs. McCaffrey."

June-bug flushed like a schoolgirl. "Jacob McCaffrey," she said, "you stop carryin' on that-a-way."

There was a moment of perfect stillness, during which something private passed between husband and wife; some elemental, unspoken language known only to them. Love them both though he did, Gage felt a brief and acidic sting of envy, looking on. Once, fool that he was, he'd thought he had that same affinity with Liza. He'd trusted her utterly, shared the most secret, the most fragile of his dreams and, ultimately, she had betrayed him. Sided with Luke and his grandfather. No doubt, it had all been a joke to Liza, from the first, but Gage had a network of soul-scars to show for the experience, and no other kind of risk scared him the way that one did. Love, to him, was a dangerous undertaking.

But Jacob and June-bug had been married for more than forty years, and in that time they had raised and lost twin sons and faced innumerable other trials and tribulations as well. In the not too distant past, Jacob had suffered a heart condition that had nearly killed him, but they'd overcome that, too, and now the old man was as healthy as the mules that pulled coaches for the Springwater stage line. It seemed to Gage that every sorrow, every joy, had merely served to draw them closer, until their very souls were fused, one inseparable from the other.

Gage wanted what the McCaffreys had and feared with his whole heart that he would never find it. Maybe, God help him, Liza had been the only woman he would ever dare to care about, but down deep he wanted passion and fire. He wanted love.

Indeed, whatever mark he might make in the world, Gage knew he would be a failure if he did not find that one right woman. It would help like hell, he reflected grimly, if he had any idea where to look.

"Sit down and eat, both of you," June-bug commanded, breaking the spell as she reached back to untie her calico apron.

"And where's Toby run off to, just when I've got supper on the table? That boy don't stay put any better'n a basket of kittens."

Toby, the McCaffreys' fifteen-year-old foster son, was much taken with young Emma, daughter of Trey and Rachel Hargreaves, and spent most of his spare time across the road at the Hargreaves house, according to Jacob, "getting underfoot." Trey and his pretty missus didn't seem to mind, though — they nearly always had a houseful anyway, what with the two smaller children of their own and the Wainwright kids coming and going whenever they had the yen to pass some time in town.

"Toby'll be along," Jacob said. He and June-bug took their places at the table, and Gage joined them as soon as they were both seated.

Sure enough, Toby burst in while Jacob was offering the blessing, about as subtle as a snowstorm in July. The boy washed hastily and sat down next to Gage just as the resounding "amen" was raised.

"And how are Trey and Rachel keeping these days?" Jacob asked with a smile in his voice. His rugged features were as solemn as ever. "And Miss Emma, of course?"

Toby, a good-looking kid with straight blond hair and the kind of impudent manner girls always seemed to take to right off, colored a little as he took a biscuit from the platter Jacob passed his way. "They're all right," he said and, after only a moment's hesitation, helped himself to a second biscuit before handing the rest on to Gage. "I could have stayed for supper, but I told them I wouldn't miss one of Miss June-bug's meals for anything."

Gage suppressed a smile. The kid was a charmer, that was for sure.

"Did Emma wear that pretty new dress her mama and I made for her last Saturday afternoon?" June-bug asked. Her eyes were bright with affection for the boy, but he squirmed a little all the same, well aware that he was being teased, and suitably self-conscious.

"Yes, ma'am," he said, and summoned up a winning grin. "She looked mighty good, too."

"Well," said June-bug, "of course she did. As for you, Toby McCaffrey, I will expect you to be on time for supper after this just the same. It ain't good manners to make other folks wait for their victuals."

Not, Gage thought with a private smile, that they'd been going to wait.

Toby ducked his head. Abandoned by his father as a lad and found living alone in the woods by the town's first official school-marm, Rachel Hargreaves, he had been staying with the McCaffreys ever since. His father, a no-good specimen if Gage had ever heard tell of one, had tried once to reclaim his son, though not because of any paternal devotion. Instead, Mike Houghton had wanted someone to mind the horses while he and his gang robbed banks, stage-coaches, and telegraph offices. That had all been settled five years back, however, when Houghton had been killed prior to going to prison, and Toby had taken his foster parents' name as his own. Gage, arriving in town about six months later, had done the legal honors himself.

Now, probably to deflect the topic of conversation from his own penchant for the company of pretty Emma Hargreaves, Toby turned a grin on Gage. It wouldn't work as well on him or Jacob as it did with June-bug, but he had to give the kid credit for the attempt.

"Well," Toby demanded cheerfully, "did you sweet-talk the newspaper lady, tell her you were sorry about her brother dyin' and all?"

It was beginning to dawn on Gage that he had indeed been too hasty in approaching Miss Barnes about the newspaper. He and

Michael had not been friends, precisely, but he had served as Barnes's attorney, being the only one in town. As the executor of his will, he understood the state of the family's finances only too well, and he had hoped to ease the burden by purchasing the struggling business at a fair price. Apparently, though, if Toby had heard about Gage's plans, the matter must be the subject of considerable talk around Springwater.

"I guess I could have given her a bit more time to get her bearings," he admitted. *Had* he offered Miss Barnes his condolences? He didn't rightly remember, given that she'd had an effect on him similar to being butted in the belly by a ram. He might well have committed such an oversight and, worse still, he'd offered to take her infant nieces off her hands as though they were a pair of secondhand buggy wheels. As though she were incompetent to raise them.

He groaned out loud. No wonder she hadn't taken a shine to him.

"What did I say?" Toby asked in an aggrieved manner, looking from Gage to Junebug to Jacob.

"My boy," Jacob replied sagely, "you see before you a man who has just seen the error of his ways." While he imparted this wisdom, he buttered another biscuit.

Jessica would not have slept at all that second night in Springwater, except that she was utterly spent. When she awoke in the chilly light of a winter morning, feeling rested, it was to a chorus of squalling babies.

After bracing herself, she got out of bed and set her bare feet on the icy floor. Jupiter and Zeus, she thought, if she was this cold, then those poor children must be nearly frozen to death.

She hurried to the large cradle, which was situated at the foot of the bed Michael and Victoria had shared in what was now her room, and peered anxiously down at the pair of squirming, shrieking bundles tucked and swaddled in their blankets.

Both infants were fair, with wide, corn-flower-blue eyes. The one at the far end of the cradle was Mary Catherine, Jessica decided, which meant that the other must be Eleanor Lorraine. Or was it the other way around?

The babies began to scream in earnest, and at an ever-rising pitch. The tiny blue veins showed at their temples, and their round faces were bright red. Desperately Jessica grabbed up one furious niece in each arm and bounced them fitfully on her hips. "Hush, now," she pleaded, as though they were amenable to reason. "Hush."

Alma appeared at last in the doorway, just cinching the belt of her wrapper. "What a ruckus," she said with a pleased smile.

"What do they want?" Jessica asked reasonably.

Alma shook her head a couple of times, with an accompanying *tsk-tsk* sound, then came briskly over and commandeered one of the infants. "Why, they're hungry, the little rascals, and no doubt you could wring out their knickers like a dishrag."

Jessica only grew more unnerved. She had changed diapers before — yesterday, as a matter of fact — but she was temporarily stymied by the intricacies of feeding these small and wretchedly unhappy creatures.

"There's a bit of milk left," Alma said. "I've got it in a crock outside the kitchen window, but you can be sure it won't be enough to satisfy Mary Catherine and Eleanor. They have hearty appetites, little pioneers that they are."

Hearty lungs, too, Jessica thought, with a mixture of frustration and pride. Helplessly, she bounced the remaining twin — whoever it was — in a vain effort to lend comfort. "What are we going to do?"

"I," said Alma, "am going to put dry diapers on these babies and then give them

46

what's left of the milk. You, meanwhile, had better get yourself dressed and see if you can't borrow a bucketful from the Mc-Caffreys. They keep a cow, you know, since they have to feed all those people who pass through on the stage."

Jessica laid the infant on the bed — as far as she could tell, neither of the twins had taken a breath since they'd commenced to raising the roof — and groped her way somewhat awkwardly into yesterday's clothes. She had not as yet had a chance to unpack her trunks, let alone launder her well-worn travel garments. "Borrow from the McCaffreys? I was sure I saw a general store —"

Alma sniffed. "You did, but That Woman who runs the place is no better than she should be, if you know what I mean. Essie Farham says That Woman's set her cap for Essie's own husband."

Jessica sighed. She meant to reserve judgment where That Woman was concerned, since she'd almost certainly been accused of such indiscretions herself after she fled the Covington house in disgrace, and wrongfully so.

For the moment, however, it seemed easier to comply with Alma's wishes and approach the McCaffreys for help. Michael had said, many times, that God never put a kinder pair of souls on this earth than those two.

Matters at hand were far too pressing to allow for further reflection. Hastily Jessica pinned up her hair, splashed her face with water cold enough to sting, donned her blue woolen cloak, and went out, making her way cautiously down the ice-covered stairs to the sidewalk.

The snow had stopped, and the sun was shining brightly, but the wind was bitterly cold and it was hard going, trudging through the drifts that hid the road from view.

Jessica paused, looking one way and then the other. The Springwater station, if she remembered correctly, was beyond the Brimstone Saloon and the doctor's office, at the far end of the road. She had arrived there by coach — could it have been just the day before? — but so much had happened since then. She'd expected to be greeted by Michael, all too recently widowed; instead, she'd been met by one Jacob McCaffrey, who had told her quietly that her brother was gone, that they'd buried him just a week before, beside his young wife.

She supposed she'd gone into a state of shock then — she didn't remember being escorted to the humble quarters over the *Gazette*, where Alma had been doing her best to care for two orphaned infants who seemed somehow to know that they'd been left behind.

Like Michael and I, she thought, as she marched through the deep snow. She didn't often think about her childhood, but the memories had a tendency to creep in when her guard was down. She didn't remember her mother or her father — she'd been so young when they died — but on rainy days, when they were both small, Michael had told her long and complicated stories about them. Even then she'd known they were mostly made up, those tales, but they'd been a great comfort all the same.

Samuel Barnes, their uncle and guardian, had run a small newspaper, and he'd expected Michael to follow in his footsteps and take over the business when the time came. Instead, Michael had decided to head west, and a breach had opened between the two men that was never to be mended. Uncle Samuel had died of a heart ailment only a month after Michael's departure.

Jessica peered through the snowy dazzle; best she keep her mind on fetching milk for the twins. The station was in sight now, and even though the sun was shining fit to blind

49

a person, there were still lamps glowing in some of the windows.

Jessica was careful not to glance toward the churchyard and Michael's grave. In the frigid, blue-gold light of that mid-January moment, the loss seemed even greater than the day before, when she'd stood beside his marker, the pain even more ferocious.

She lifted her chin, and each breath she drew burned her nostrils, throat, and lungs like an inhalation of dry fire. She would not give up the babies, no matter what — but perhaps she had been too quick to turn down Mr. Calloway's offer to buy the newspaper. With the proceeds of the sale, she could have set up a modest household, telling people she was a widow, and would have made a proper home for the children.

Jessica sighed. If she'd had only herself to think about, she would have gone to Denver or San Francisco and found herself another position as a companion, for she was well-qualified and had a fine letter of recommendation from the late Mrs. Covington, despite the problems with that woman's son. Finding work with infant twins in tow, however, was quite another matter.

She'd learned, to her sorrow, that people often favored gossip over truth, and even if she'd been able to find employers who would accept the babies, too, there would inevitably be speculation, whatever her story. Better just to stay in Springwater, where folks knew what had happened, and might be expected to look kindly on a young woman trying to keep what remained of her family together.

Before she'd reached the steps of the station's narrow porch, the door swung open and a smiling woman appeared in the chasm. The scents of fresh coffee, bacon, and burning firewood wafted out to beckon Jessica inside, and her stomach rumbled audibly.

"You must be June-bug," she said, attempting to respond with a smile that kept slipping off her lips.

"I am at that," June-bug replied. "And you would be Miss Jessica Barnes of St. Louis, Missouri. Come on in and set a spell. I could do with a good visit. Rachel's so busy these days, with all those young'uns, and Savannah helps her husband most days. He's the doc, you know. Miranda lives way out of town, and so does Evangeline, and I get right lonesome for female company."

Jessica longed to accept the invitation, and she was eager to hear more about each of the women Mrs. McCaffrey had mentioned, but she had her hungry nieces to think about. Indeed, she'd have little time for visiting, most likely, between them and the newspaper, before the twins grew up and got married.

"I've come to buy milk," she blurted. "The babies are screaming like banshees."

That announcement was enough to set all the wheels and cogs of Springwater station in motion. Toby and Jacob, June-bug informed her, had ridden out to meet the stagecoach, since it was overdue, and she had her hands full with the baking, but that didn't mean they couldn't help a neighbor, no sir.

Before she knew precisely what had happened, Jessica found herself leading a borrowed cow down the middle of Center Street.

Alma stood pop-eyed on the wooden sidewalk while the babies' wails of discontent spilled down the stairs like stones toppled from a bucket. "Why," she gasped, as fresh snowflakes began to fall, "it's a *cow*."

Jessica gazed forlornly back at the beast, which was now bawling as piteously as the babies. Between that and those unceasing shrieks from upstairs, Jessica was hard put to keep from dropping the lead rope and pressing both hands to her ears. Instead, she squared her shoulders and asked, "Have you any idea how to milk this creature?"

Alma's mouth twitched — she was a rancher's wife, after all — but she laid one hand to her bosom in the profoundest alarm. "My, no!" she cried, and even though Jessica knew it was a lie, there wasn't much she could do. Alma was, in fact, gazing past Jessica and the cow, toward the telegraph office across the street.

"Well," replied Jessica, after a distracted glance in that direction, in which she glimpsed a shadow at the window, "we'd best reason it out, hadn't we?" She walked around the animal's steaming, twitching bulk. "Do fetch me a bucket," she said, in a tone that sounded as decisive as it was false. "And then go inside and shut the door before those poor children catch their deaths!" She was sorry for this thoughtless reference the moment she'd uttered it; certainly, death was not a subject to be spoken of lightly.

Alma nodded resolutely, and hurried back inside. Shortly she appeared with the bucket that had contained their drinking water.

Jessica thanked her without conviction, holding the empty pail in both arms while she pondered the bovine dilemma. She heard the door close behind Alma, heard through it the continuing angry complaints of the twins. She did not notice that she had drawn an audience — early revelers from the saloon — until she'd seated herself somewhat awkwardly on the high edge of the sidewalk and set the bucket beneath the cow's swollen udder.

Tentatively she reached out, gripped a wrinkled teat, and just as quickly withdrew. This raised raucous howls of delight from the seedy spectators.

Jessica stood up, hands resting on her hips, and glowered at the men over the cow's shuddering back. "If there was a gentleman among you," she said forcefully, "he would offer to help!"

"We herd cows, ma'am," one of the wasters called back. "We don't milk 'em." Another round of merriment followed, as though the man had said something uproariously funny.

"Idiots," Jessica murmured.

It was then that the door of the telegraph office opened behind the little crowd of drovers, and Mr. Calloway pushed his way through, albeit good-naturedly. He was dressed in a most dapper fashion, considering that this was early morning in a frontier town, and he grinned at Jessica just as if they'd gotten off to an auspicious beginning. Tugging at the brim of his fancy black hat, he crossed the road to face her over the broad expanse of the McCaffrey milk cow. "Allow me, ma'am," he said, and came around to take up Jessica's former seat on the plank walkway.

"Thank you," Jessica said, though stiffly. She wasn't sure what to make of Mr. Calloway and his admittedly chivalrous gesture, not after all Michael had written about him, both in his letters and in the *Gazette*. She did not often revise her opinions once they were set, but in the case of this man it seemed an exception might be called for — however temporary it might be.

The milk began to squirt noisily into the bucket, foaming and warmly fragrant, and Jessica wanted to weep, she was so relieved. She merely sniffled, as it happened, watching the milking process carefully for future reference. The cowboys, evidently bored, mounted their horses and rode off, spoiling the pristine ribbon of snow that was Center Street.

All around, the town began to come to life — the general store was opened for business, and the bell in the tower of the little brick schoolhouse — a recent addition to the town, according to Michael's letters — began to chime. A wagon made its way past, driven by a smiling man with his collar pulled up around his neck. The woman at his side smiled, too, and waved as the rig paused. Two gangly, red-haired boys, tall as men, leaped out of the wagon bed and immediately began pelting each other with hastily constructed snowballs.

"Mornin', Gage," the man called affably, showing no apparent surprise to see his friend milking a cow in the center of town. He ignored the boys, clearly used to their rough-and-tumble ways.

"Landry," Gage called back in greeting, as the other man got down and lifted a smaller boy from the seat. Until then, the child had been hidden between the two adults. He was a chubby little bundle, with red cheeks and fair curly hair peeking out from beneath his stocking cap. "Hello, Miranda. That you, Isaiah? Lord, you've gotten so big, I hardly recognized you."

The child beamed in response to Gage's remark. Isaiah. Such a big name, Jessica thought fondly, for such a little boy.

The woman waved, but her gaze was fixed on Jessica now, betraying an intense but not unfriendly curiosity. *Miranda.* Hadn't Junebug mentioned her, just that morning, when she had gone to the station for milk?

Still broken inside over the loss of her brother, but equally determined not to make a public display of her sorrow, Jessica summoned up what she hoped was a polite expression and waggled the fingers of her right hand in reply to the other woman's greeting.

Miranda's husband hiked Isaiah up onto his sturdy shoulders with an exaggerated grunt of effort, and started toward the school, whistling happily. Miranda turned on the seat and Jessica saw that she was not only holding a blanketed bundle that must surely have contained a small child, she was hugely pregnant, as well.

Jessica felt a deep and fearfully elemental stirring inside, sudden and sharp-edged, and realized with a start that it was simple envy. Why this should be, she could not fathom — she had two infant nieces to raise, albeit without the help of a husband, and no need of more responsibility. And yet, for the first time in a long while, she let herself feel the old longing for a home, a mate, a family of her own.

Watching Mr. Covington in action had caused her to vow never to leave herself open to the sort of pain and humiliation so many women suffered at the hands of their men, but seeing such happiness as Landry and Miranda enjoyed made her want to start over, with all new thoughts and beliefs and attitudes.

"We are really sorry about Michael and Victoria," Miranda said, holding the bundle close against her and draping the edge of her cloak over it. "They were nice folks."

Jessica's gaze strayed involuntarily in the direction of the churchyard, where Michael and his pretty bride were buried, side by side, beneath rocks and dirt and drifts of glittering snow. "Thank you," she said, though she wasn't sure she'd spoken loudly enough for Miranda to hear.

Gage went on milking, humming happily to himself, his hat pushed to the back of his head. The milk made sweet steam in the cold, crisp air.

Chattering children began to converge on the schoolhouse from every direction — the big house down the road, just across the way from the stagecoach station, the row of more modest places beyond the church, the surrounding countryside. The man Gage called Landry — whether that was his first name or his last Jessica could not guess — came out of the school without the little boy and crossed the street to slap the McCaffrey cow affectionately on one flank. Up close, Jessica could see that he was very good-looking, with a mischievous curve to his mouth. His hazel eyes sobered, though, as he regarded her.

"That was a shame, your brother and sister-in-law passing on the way they did. We're real sorry, and if there's anything you need, you just speak up. Folks around Springwater surely do like to be helpful whenever they can."

"Thank you," Jessica murmured, head bowed.

Gage had finished his task at last; he rose and handed the bucket to Jessica. She hoped he could see her gratitude in her eyes, for she was incapable of speaking. Her losses were still so fresh that any reference to them threatened her composure. She did, however, manage a nod.

Mr. Calloway spoke with a gentleness that was quite nearly her undoing. "I'll see that Tilly here gets back to her stall down at the station. You'd best tend to those hungry babies."

Jessica nodded again and fled.

Chapter

3

Clasping the bucket handle with the bare and cold-stiffened fingers of both hands, Jessica turned and hurried toward the relative solace of the upstairs apartments. The babies, all cried out, had settled into sorrowful hiccups, while Alma sat in the chair by the window, rocking them both with a sort of wry desperation. "I gave them what milk there was, and they howled for more," she said.

"Here," Jessica said, indicating the heavy bucket she carried. "We can give them all they want."

When the milk had been strained through a clean dishtowel — it barely required heating, being still warm from the cow — Jessica refilled the two glass bottles and settled down to feeding Mary Catherine, while Alma did the same with little Eleanor.

Or was it the other way around? No matter. Jessica's life as a mother had well and truly begun, and while she was over-whelmed, the fact was not without its com-pensations. As she held that baby, a certain special warmth stole into her heart and set up residence forever; in that odd, transcen-dent instant, both children became her own, as surely as if she'd carried them in her womb.

She began to weep, making no sound at all, and Alma, without a word, laid little El-eanor, bottle and all, in the crook of Jessica's right arm, that she might hold them both. From that moment on, there was never any question: Jessica would do virtually any-thing for those babies.

Jacob extended one time- and work-gnarled hand to accept the lead rope when Gage brought home the cow. A grin flick-ered in the old man's dark eyes. "I hear you've taken to doin' the milkin' of a mornin', Gage," he said in his unmistakable baritone. "I reckon June-bug should've fig-ured Miss Barnes didn't know how to manage a chore like that and sent Trey or somebody on over there. Toby and I went out to meet the stage."

Gage chuckled and rubbed his chin — his beard was coming in and he'd forgotten to shave that morning, for thinking about

61

Jessica Barnes and what ought to be done about her. He'd watched her slowly trudging down the road toward the station, and seen her return soon after leading the cow. He'd enjoyed watching her futile efforts for a while, but in the end simple chivalry — not to mention the fact that he could hear those children hollering with hunger from all the way across the street — had forced him to go out and help. "You suppose she knows any more about running a newspaper than she does about milking a cow?"

Jacob led old Tilly into the barn, which was redolent with the singular and not unpleasant smells of animals and hay, and secured her in a stall, where grain and fresh water awaited. As usual, he took his time answering. " 'Bout as much as you do, I guess," he observed dryly, and at some length. There was just the hint of a sparkle in his eyes.

Gage took off his hat and swept one hand through his hair. No point in bragging that he'd been raised in a press room; it didn't have any bearing on the conversation anyhow. "Maybe that's so," he allowed, with a testy edge to his voice, "but there's one thing you're forgetting: she's a woman."

Jacob gave a low whistle of exclamation

and ambled toward the barn door, rummaging for tobacco and a pipe as he went. June-bug did not permit the use of such inside the station, for she believed smoking to be an unhealthy and despicable habit.

"If I was you," Jacob said, taking up where the whistle had left off, "I'd be careful about sayin' things like that. We've got some spirited women in these parts — I can think of five or six that would skin you and nail up your hide just for talking that way."

Gage let the remark pass unchallenged; after all, it was true. Springwater was indeed populated by a lot of strong-minded females, and as far as he could see, Jessica Barnes would fit in just fine. He wondered what lucky and accursed man would be the one to rope her in — probably some farmer, who'd have her milking cows like an expert in no time at all.

For some reason, he found the idea distasteful. Some women weren't meant for such chores, and the prissy, stiff-necked Miss Barnes was surely one of them.

"You gonna tell her?" Jacob prodded, drawing on his pipe. A wreath of smoke rose like a halo over his head.

Gage was beginning to feel a mite short-tempered, despite the cheerful mood he'd enjoyed earlier. "Tell her what?" he shot back, though he damn well knew the answer. Michael Barnes had owed him money — a sizable amount, as it happened — and he'd put up the newspaper for collateral. Offering to buy the place was an outright act of charity, given that he could have claimed it, with the full blessing of the law, at any time. Somehow, looking in Jessica Barnes's eyes, he just hadn't been able to get the words out.

Jacob shrugged those bull-brawny shoulders of his, and snow settled like shimmering feathers on his dark hair. "It's your money," he said, and walked away toward the station house, still puffing on his pipe.

Disgruntled, Gage took himself back to his office. He shared the chilly, cramped space with C. W. Brody, the Western Union man, who lived upstairs. A widower in his late forties, C.W. was tapping industriously at the telegraph key when Gage stepped inside to hang up his hat for the second time that morning. He kept his coat on, however, and crossed the room to stuff a few chunks of wood into the potbellied stove. Rubbing his palms together in an attempt to get his bloodstream flowing again, he took to wondering if Jessica and Miss Alma and those two little babies were warm enough.

Landry and Jacob and Trey Hargreaves

had laid in a cord or two of seasoned pine and birch logs back when Barnes had taken sick, but they'd left the task of splitting and stacking for later, having plenty of work of their own to do, and had never gotten back to it.

C.W. stopped his clicking and cleared his throat. "Here I thought you was nothin' but a fancy city boy," he said with amusement. "Turns out you're a hand with a milk cow and not too proud to show it."

Gage tightened his jaw for a moment and glanced at the large wooden clock affixed to the far wall. His first clients of the day, the Parrishes, were due in fifteen minutes. After he'd seen them and broken the news about the babies and all, he'd go over and chop some of that wood piled behind the newspaper office. It wasn't that he wanted to see Miss Barnes again, he assured himself, though he had to admit just looking at her face made him feel like he was walking a tightwire a hundred feet above the ground. No, it was his civic duty to chop that wood, and that was all there was to it.

He poured a mug full of coffee from the enamel pot on the stove and took a thoughtful sip before deciding he'd let C.W.'s comment dangle long enough. "Even rich people keep cows," he allowed, a little sharply, before heading into his office and closing the door firmly behind him. The truth was, he hadn't learned how to perform that particular lowly task until he got to Springwater. While his house was being constructed — the house he seldom used, because he'd built it for a woman who was never going to show up — he'd boarded at the station, and he'd helped Jacob and Toby with the daily round of chores. It was during that time that he'd developed a lasting affection for June-bug McCaffrey and her cooking.

Savannah arrived on time, though without the doc, who was probably busy stitching some cowpuncher back together, either out on the range or over at his office. He was a respected man, Prescott Parrish; he'd earned the esteem of the whole town over and over again, most recently by operating on young Christabel Johnson's twisted foot. He'd put it straight, and now she could walk as well as anyone else, thanks to him. She'd blossomed into a lovely, if somewhat shy, young woman who hoped to teach at the Springwater School one day, after attending normal school back in Pennsylvania.

"I'm sorry," Gage said, after he'd explained to Savannah that Miss Barnes meant to raise her nieces herself, despite the obvious disadvantages — such as not being married. He hoped she had money of her own, because Michael sure as hell hadn't left her any.

Savannah took the announcement well, though a certain sadness shone in her eyes. She and the doc had prospered, due to Trey Hargreaves giving them shares in his silver mine early on, in partial payment for Savannah's half of the Brimstone Saloon. They lived across the street from Gage's empty place and had a child of their own, but they'd wanted a big family, and it was beginning to look as if that wouldn't happen.

It was an ironic situation; Pres had helped so many other people since coming to Springwater, but this was evidently beyond even him. They'd built that big white house of theirs two years back, expecting to need the room, but now there were just the three of them rattling around the place like beans in a barrel. Sometimes the Johnson girl stayed with them, to help with the little one and the washing and cooking and such, but of course that wasn't the same thing as having a houseful of kids.

"I'm not surprised," Savannah said, after pondering Jessica's decision in silence for a few moments. "I'd do the same thing in her place. I guess I was hoping she'd turn out to

67

be another sort of woman."

Gage settled back in his creaky office chair, tenting his fingers beneath his chin. "Oh?" he prompted.

Savannah offered a shaky smile. "Victoria told me she was a spinster — a companion or a governess or something like that, that she'd traveled. That she was used to city life and to living in big houses, whether they were her own or not. It didn't sound like she was the sort to take in babies, even if they did belong to her brother."

Savannah looked so despairing just then that Gage wanted to reach across the desk and touch her hand. He didn't, though, because he knew she was fragile, and trying hard to hold up. Sympathy could only weaken her.

He spoke gruffly. "There are plenty of orphans in this world, Savannah. I could wire a friend of mine, down in San Francisco —"

She shook her head and rose hastily to her feet, her chair scraping against the plain wooden floor. "No," she said, and tried to smile again, though she couldn't seem to manage it a second time. "No," she repeated, more calmly. "Pres is right. We've got each other, and our little Beatrice. Maybe it's just plain greedy to want anything more."

With that, she took up her cloak and rushed out of the office, leaving Gage to gaze thoughtfully after her.

He was a kind man, the doctor, dark-haired and handsome, with few words to spare and a very serious countenance. Dropping his stethoscope into a battered kit bag, he studied Jessica thoughtfully, there in the tiny parlor that stood directly over the still and silent press on which Michael had so proudly printed issue after issue of the weekly *Springwater Gazette*. "Alma's homesick for her house and her husband," he said quietly. "She'll be fine."

"And the twins?" Jessica asked. Because the doctor was there making an impromptu call on Alma, who suffered occasional palpitations, Jessica had enjoined him to examine the babies, as well, just to be on the safe side. After all, both their parents had died recently, and it was her deepest fear that they too would contract whatever malady had caused Michael's death. They were a vital part of her now, like arms and legs, and she did not know what she'd do without them.

He grinned, taking Jessica by surprise, as he'd seemed so dour before. She'd supposed his reticence was partly due to the fact that he and his wife had wished to adopt the twins as their own, but now she decided it was simply his nature to be solemn. No doubt, as a doctor, he'd seen a great deal of suffering in his time, and that would cast a shadow over anyone's spirit. "They're fine," he said. "If all my patients were as lively as that pair, I'd have to go into another line of work."

Jessica found herself liking this man, and expected to like his wife, too, for all that she'd feared them a little up until now. They were an integral part of Springwater, after all, and could surely count on the support of the community, while she was new in town, a stranger to all of them. "Won't you stay for tea?" she asked. Alma was lying down, the babies were sleeping, filled once again with milk from the McCaffreys' cow, and there was nothing at hand to distract Jessica from the facts of her life — she was alone, essentially, with two infants depending on her for everything, for Alma's husband was sure to come for her soon. The future seemed bleak in that low moment, and full of struggle.

"Can't stay," the doctor said regretfully, snapping the bag shut. "I've got half a dozen more calls to make before dark."

Jessica wrung her hands. "I wanted to ask about my brother and — and, of course, Victoria. How it was for them. . . ."

70

He looked at her with a directness that she appreciated. "Victoria hemorrhaged after having the babies, and try though we might, Savannah and I couldn't stop the bleeding. She lapsed into unconsciousness and was gone within four hours." He paused, then sighed. "Michael fell over in the newspaper office one afternoon, ran a high fever that night, and died the next morning. And yes, Miss Barnes — I did everything I could to save them. Everything."

She blushed. She hadn't been going to ask, but apparently the discerning Dr. Parrish had seen the question in her eyes. "It'll be a disappointment to your wife, not to be able to adopt the babies," she said, and then wondered why she'd spoken of the matter at all. The decision had been made, and would be abided by. The news didn't seem to surprise the doctor.

"Yes," he answered readily. "Savannah longs for more children, and we haven't been able to have them."

"I'm sorry."

He simply nodded. Then, with a brief word of farewell, he was gone.

Jessica stood in the center of the parlor, fighting back another swell of terrible loneliness, and it was a while before she heard the steady *thwack-thwack* coming from somewhere out back.

Moving slowly to the window, she looked down to see Gage Calloway, coatless in the thickening snow, his sleeves rolled up to reveal solid forearms, splitting firewood with powerful swings of an ax. Something about him made Jessica's heart surge up into her throat and swell there, cutting off her breath.

As if he sensed that she was there watching him, he looked up, and their eyes met. He grinned and paused long enough to wave one hand. Jessica actually felt lightheaded when he did that, but she attributed the response to fatigue and grief.

With some effort, she managed to raise the sill, and leaned out through the opening. The cold bit into every pore of her body with teeth like tiny needles. "What are you doing?" she demanded. It was all bluster and bravado; she could not let herself forget that this man, though posing as her friend, had been a foe to her brother. Establishing any sort of association with him would be an outright betrayal.

"What does it look like I'm doing?" he retorted, but good-naturedly. His breath was a white cloud around his head and, dear Lord, he had finely made shoulders, narrow hips, long, muscular legs. He might have strode right down off Mt. Olympus, if it weren't for his modern clothes.

Jessica was exasperated, not only with him, but with herself. She huffed out an impatient sigh. "If you expect to ingratiate yourself to me and thus persuade me to sell the *Gazette*," she said, "you are wasting your time."

His grin faded, and he shook his head. "You are one prickly female," he said. "*Ingratiate* myself to you? Why, I'd sooner cozy up to a porcupine!"

"Why don't you?" she retorted. It was so much easier, so much safer, not to like him.

He sighed. "I'm not trying to do anything but make sure you have enough firewood to keep warm. Around Springwater, we call that being neighborly."

Stuck for an answer, Jessica drew back from the window and slammed it down hard enough to set the heavy glass to rattling. Below, Mr. Calloway went back to his woodchopping, and it did seem to Jessica that he was wielding that ax of his with a mite more force than before.

Early the next morning the McCaffrey boy, Toby, knocked at the door with a beguiling grin and a bucket of fresh milk, strained and separated and ready to be heated for the babies' bottles. "Miss Junebug says you ought to come to the station for a visit first chance you get," he announced happily. His nose and the tops of his ears were red with cold, and his blue eyes fairly gleamed with that special exuberance that is reserved for the very young. "You're to bring the babies, too."

Jessica accepted the milk gratefully, promised to pay a call on Mrs. McCaffrey before the end of the week, and watched as Toby descended the stairs, taking two at a time. She was closing the door when Alma came out of her room; the apartment was deliciously warm, thanks to the plenitude of firewood, and the twins were still sleeping cozily in their shared cradle at the foot of Jessica's bed. There was time to warm the milk, and the soft, quiet light of the new snow trimming the windowpanes lent the place an almost festive air.

Alma went to stand before the fire, diminutive in her sturdy woolen wrapper and slippers. "My Pete will be here to fetch me soon. I reckon he's gotten word of your arrival by now."

Jessica merely nodded. She was not looking forward to caring for the babies by herself, but she would manage somehow.

She was intelligent and capable, and she could learn.

"You don't seem to get on with Gage Calloway very well," Alma observed. "He's a fine man, you know."

Jessica stiffened slightly. No doubt Alma knew, as the rest of the town surely did, of the animosity between Mr. Calloway and her brother. It would not serve to point out the obvious. "He must have some fatal flaw," she remarked instead.

The other woman faced her squarely, and her expression was entirely serious. "He doesn't," she said flatly. "Comes from a fine family down in San Francisco. Folks with money and breeding. Lives in that big house across the street from Doc and Savannah's place, all by himself. People say he built it for a woman who broke his heart."

Broken heart aside — that could happen to anyone, after all — it figured that Gage came from a rich family. He was used to privilege, used to squashing people — like Michael — who got in his way. Hadn't she seen Mr. Covington and his friends do such things, over and over? Her rage was renewed, and it sustained her; in those moments it was all that kept her from sinking into a state of complete melancholy.

"And?" she prompted, knowing that Alma

would go on whether she was invited to or not.

"You could do worse for yourself," Alma said bluntly. Once she finally got around to making her point, she closed right in for the kill. "Than Gage Calloway, I mean."

Jessica laid one hand to her bosom, fingers splayed. "Good heavens, Alma," she exclaimed, careful, for the babies' sakes, to keep her voice moderate. "I barely know the man." *But I know enough.* She saw by her friend's expression that she was unconvinced. "And in any case, he has not shown the first sign of wanting to court me, let alone proposed. You have taken notice of that, haven't you?"

"Bullfeathers. It's plain to see that he's taken with you. Didn't he milk the cow yesterday? Didn't he chop all that wood?"

Jessica was losing her patience. "For heaven's sake, Alma, he was merely being kind." Gage Calloway could milk cows and chop wood for a thousand years and it would never make up for what he'd done to Michael.

"Every man in this town is kind," Alma exclaimed, as the babies began, first one and then both, to lament their empty stomachs and wet diapers. "But you didn't see any of *them* over here looking for ways to be

76

helpful, did you?"

He wants the newspaper, Jessica reminded herself, for she found that she was weakening a little under the onslaught of Alma's conviction. "Please prepare the bottles," she said as the twins raised their howling to a new pitch. "I will see to the rest."

The next hour was occupied with caring for the infants, but once they'd been burped and bathed and bundled up for another round of sleep, Jessica could no longer escape the inevitable. She put on a shawl, went downstairs, and opened the door of the newspaper office.

It was dusty inside, and bitterly cold, but the place still gave the impression that Michael had just stepped out on some brief errand. His ink-stained printer's apron hung on a peg beside the door, precisely where he'd left it. His visor lay on the desktop, along with a box of type, carefully laid out.

Jessica blinked and ran her fingertips lightly across the smooth metal letters, the last issue, surely, of the *Springwater Gazette,* as published and edited by Michael Barnes. It took a moment to make out the headline, since the type was set backwards, but when she did, she wanted to weep: CALLOWAY: THE MAN WHO WOULD BUY SPRINGWATER. She rounded the press to read the rest of the article, in which Michael maintained that citizens should not be misled by Mr. Calloway's engaging nature and seeming generosity. He was, Michael claimed, a wolf in sheep's clothing, and taking office as mayor was only the first step in a plan that would, if unchecked, take him all the way to the territorial governor's office.

Jessica frowned. Gage Calloway had political aspirations beyond Springwater. Had he tried to put Michael out of business simply to silence him, to quell articles like this one?

She reminded herself yet again that Calloway still entertained hopes of persuading her to sell the *Gazette*, clear as she'd been in refusing. Publishing a newspaper, even in such a sparsely populated area, would give him significant influence; as a rule, people tended to believe what they read, simply because it had been set in type and printed. She must be wary, on her guard, and never let herself be taken in by his charm.

Jessica sighed. She hadn't the first glimmer of how to run that ancient press Michael had so treasured, but she had a good mind and, given time, she would figure it out. After pushing up the sleeves of her practical calico dress, she fetched some wood from the covered bin that stood out back beneath the broad eaves, and started a fire in the small stove in one corner of the room. When the frost melted from the floors and the cold receded somewhat, Jessica circled the great, cumbersome press, studying it thoughtfully.

After a while, when it seemed to her that the construction of the machine made at least a little bit of sense, she set the type box where it seemed it ought to go, inked the rollers, and turned the heavy hand crank at one side of the looming iron mechanism. The paper, housed on a great cylinder, wrinkled and then jammed the works.

Muttering, Jessica put on Michael's apron and turned the full and formidable force of her will upon the task at hand. By that time the following week, she vowed silently — and fiercely — she would put out an issue of the *Gazette*, however humble it might be.

He paused on the sidewalk, heedless of the bitter Montana wind sweeping across the range and straight down Springwater's main street, watching as Jessica labored over the recalcitrant press. She was covered in ink, smudged and splotched and shining with the stuff, and he didn't think he'd ever seen a lovelier sight in the whole of his life.

He supposed he ought to go in there and

show her how to manage the simple but stubborn machine — his grandfather published one of the largest newspapers in California, after all, and he'd virtually grown up, along with his half-brother, in the midst of the enterprise, an ink monkey by association — but the plain truth was that he was scared to approach her, feeling the way he did right then. His reason, highly developed, told him she was the wrong sort of woman for him, willful and prickly; he'd fallen for that sort of woman once, and look where that had landed him. What he needed was a sweet, pliant wife, one who needed protecting.

His heart, on the other hand, had a different opinion entirely.

He stood there for a time, torn between courage and cowardice, hope and fear, and then moved on. Reason had prevailed over more tender sentiments, but he couldn't exactly have said he was relieved, and a part of him, some reckless, rebellious portion of his spirit, stayed behind, with Jessica Barnes.

It was getting dark when Jessica finally gave up her efforts to produce one coherent page of copy — for the time being, at least — and dragged herself upstairs. Alma, bless her heart, had a simple supper of eggs and toasted bread at the ready, and the babies were sleeping soundly, blissful in their innocence. It was fortunate, Jessica thought, that they couldn't know they were at the mercy of a spinster aunt with nothing to offer them save a pile of crumpled newsprint.

"Look at you," Alma said with a little laugh as she steered Jessica to the table and set a plate in front of her. "Why, a body would hardly recognize you, under all that ink!"

It required a supreme effort just to lift her fork; Jessica simply wasn't up to idle conversation.

"What you need," Alma went on cheerfully, "is a nice hot bath. Wouldn't that be a fine thing?"

Jessica wanted to weep at the mere prospect. When had she last enjoyed such a luxury? Not since she'd left the Covington mansion in St. Louis, certainly, where she'd shared a bathroom with several of the maids.

She contrived to nod once, in order to let Alma know she'd heard, then swallowed an exhausted sob along with a bite of warm, buttered bread.

Alma was bustling about with sudden and rather alarming resolve. "Nothing like a good, hot bath to restore body and soul. Yes, siree. I'd like to go back home knowing you're strong and hearty, and well able to look after these babies."

Jessica tried to protest — Alma was not young, however energetic she might be feeling at the moment, and the setting out of a tub, the fetching and heating of water, were hard and heavy tasks.

For all of that, nothing would sway Alma from her quest, and by the time Jessica had finished her supper and washed her plate, fork, and knife, the older woman had dragged a round copper tub from the pantry to the hearth in the parlor, where a lively fire blazed. After emptying the stove reservoir and the two buckets of drinking water to serve her purpose, Alma finally ran down. Jessica, somewhat revived by the meal, took over for her, carrying steaming kettles to the tub.

At last, the bath was ready. A towel had been found, and a bar of lilac-scented soap that had been Victoria's. Jessica dimmed the last lamp to a faint flicker, undressed, and stepped into the tub, lowering herself into the water with a sigh of contentment. In that lulling, suspended state, the days ahead did not seem so overwhelmingly difficult as before. She knew, in those moments and thereafter, that even if she did not succeed brilliantly, she could at least *manage.* She could and would make a good and happy life for herself and her nieces, and devil take the plain fact that she wasn't sure how to go about any of it.

She would face down Michael's enemy and prevail. Her brother would, she thought, as she drifted off into a brief, sweet sleep, have been very proud of her.

Emma Hargreaves presented herself at the door of the *Gazette*'s humble office the next day, right after school let out. She was a beautiful girl, fifteen or sixteen, Jessica supposed, and the lively agility of her mind showed in her dark eyes and in each of the myriad expressions that played upon her face.

"I've come to help you print the newspaper," the girl announced, removing her cloak and hanging it carefully beside Michael's printer's apron. Apparently, it had not crossed her mind that her offer might be refused.

Jessica saw no reason to delay the inevitable, but she took care to speak gently, for she liked Emma already and did not wish to discourage her. "I'm sorry," she said. "I'm afraid I can't afford to hire help just now."

Emma beamed, unfazed. "Oh, you needn't pay me," she said happily. "My pa has shares in a silver mine, the Jupiter and Zeus, so I don't need money. I just want to write stories and work the machine and all like that."

It took Jessica a moment to assimilate the implications of such an offer. The girl could hardly be more inept than she herself — perhaps between them, they might actually print the news, sell advertising, and get the business to turning a profit.

Emma did not wait for a reply — indeed, she was bent over, peering into the mechanism attached to the paper rollers. Jessica had still not mastered this demon's device.

"I think this is stuck, this tiny part here," the girl mused, poking a finger into the small but baffling system of gears. There was a metallic *click* and Emma straightened, smiling broadly again. "It ought to be fine now. May I work the lever?"

Jessica gestured for her to go ahead, feeling skeptical and hopeful and a little indignant, all of a piece.

There was a shrill, grinding sound, and then the roller began to turn and the page of type Michael himself had set was impressed upon a wide sheet of paper.

Jessica tore the page off and stared at it in

delighted amazement. "How did you do that?"

Emma shrugged modestly. "I used to come by and watch Mr. Barnes print the paper whenever I could. He published one of my poems once — it was about a wolf."

Jessica put out an ink-stained hand. "You're hired," she said.

Later that week Alma's husband arrived, driving a buckboard, and collected her. She glowed with happiness at the prospect of going home, even as she wept to leave the babies.

"Why, they might be grown women before I see them again," she sniffled, settling into the wagon box.

"Now, Alma, don't take on," Pete scolded fondly. He was a big, rugged man, probably handsome in his youth, and he clearly loved his wife.

"I'll bring them to see you," Jessica vowed in a rash moment, having no earthly idea what such a trip might involve. "I swear I will."

Alma took her at her word and, as quickly as that, she was gone, rattling away toward home.

Unable to face being alone just then, Jessica put on her best afternoon dress, did up her hair, and proceeded to pay the promised call on June-bug McCaffrey, at the Springwater station. It was quite an enterprise, given that she was taking the twins along with her. They made two great, bulky bundles in her arms as she high-stepped her way through the hard-crusted, glittering snow.

The other woman greeted her with a cry of delight, immediately claiming one of the babies for herself. "Why, just look at this precious little smidgen!" she beamed. "And here's her sister. I declare, in twenty years' time, they'll have broken every heart in Springwater."

Warmed by June-bug's cheerful reception, Jessica smiled. Perhaps she might fit in here after all, one day. She'd just have to stay out of Gage Calloway's way as much as possible.

June-bug bustled to make beds for the babies by stuffing blankets into wooden freight boxes and gently setting the children inside. They cooed happily, as though they too felt welcome at the Springwater station.

"Sit down and I'll make you some tea," June-bug commanded, while Jessica stood awkwardly in the middle of the room, unsure of what to do next. She'd been one step above a servant for all her adult life, and she wasn't sure how to go about being entertained. "Did Alma get on toward home?"

"She's gone," Jessica said, a little forlornly, and took a seat in one of the chairs near the fireplace.

June-bug merely nodded, busy at the stove with the teakettle, and went right on chatting. "Jacob says the pond down by the spring is froze over solid. There'll be a bonfire there tomorrow night, and skating, too. I hope you'll bundle up these dear little babies and come join the fun."

Jessica did not point out that she was, for all practical intents and purposes, in mourning. Perhaps it was due, at least in part, to the fact that she knew Michael would not approve of such withdrawal. She'd known all along that he would have wanted his life to be remembered and celebrated, not the single day and hour of his death.

"I haven't any skates," she said, at a loss for other conversation.

June-bug, still busy at the stove, was undaunted. "I do believe Victoria owned a pair." Her lovely, vibrant face darkened, if only for a moment, when she looked back at Jessica over one shoulder. "Poor girl. She was never very hearty, but Lord knows, she tried."

Jessica frowned a little, puzzled. "Tried?" she echoed.

June-bug gave a weighty sigh. "To please Michael, I mean," she said, frowning reflectively. "Her heart wasn't really in it, though. Livin' way out here, I mean, amongst plain folks. Not that she was unfriendly, or high-nosed, or anything like that. She just didn't seem to like it here much."

Jessica had known her sister-in-law only slightly, prior to her marriage to Michael. She'd been bookish, sweet. Shy and delicate, too. Victoria had begged Michael not to go west to seek his fortune, adding her voice to Uncle Samuel's, and maybe she'd been right. If they'd stayed at home in St. Louis, if Michael had joined the family business, both of them might be alive today.

If. Jessica shook herself inwardly. Fruitless speculation, that was. What was done was done — Michael and his bride were gone, forever. It was up to her to pick up the fragments and move forward into the future, however uncertain it might be. Part of doing that was joining in community activities — like the skating party.

"Was my brother happy?" she asked, as June-bug set a tray on the small, sturdy table between the two chairs facing the fire, sat down across from Jessica, and began to pour

88

tea. "In his last days, I mean?"

June-bug reached out to pat her arm. "Why, sure he was," she replied with reassuring confidence. "Up until poor little Victoria passed on, that is. Losin' her took a lot out of him, but that's natural. He got to workin' at all hours of the day and night, but he loved those babies of his, and the newspaper, too. Oh, he had high hopes for the *Gazette,* and that's a fact."

Jessica sipped her tea and reflected silently upon her brother's lost dreams.

"You'll make a fine mother to these children, you know," June-bug said in a quiet voice, laying a hand to Jessica's shoulder. "You just wait and see."

Chapter

4

Poor as she and Michael had been, Victoria had indeed owned a pair of ice skates; probably she had brought them with her on the journey west to Montana Territory. Jessica found them hidden away in the bottom of a trunk, their blades dull and rusted, amongst a sad collection of small mementos — dried flowers from her wedding bouquet; a few letters, the paper thin as a spill of light on glass, tucked into yellow-edged envelopes; and various small baubles.

Just the sight of those simple, unassuming things, so obviously treasured, filled Jessica with guilt. She had grieved so much over Michael that she had almost forgotten to mourn Victoria, a young woman who would never watch her own babies grow, or hear them laugh, would never see another spring . . .

Jessica took a deep breath and guided her

mind in another direction. Holding the skates close against her chest, she remembered her girlhood, when she and Michael and a crowd of friends had spent winter afternoons skating on a pond not far from their uncle's house. Those had been some of the happiest times of her life; she'd felt free while skating, exhilarated by her own smooth velocity and the brisk caress of the wind.

Soon enough, though, her thoughts turned back to Victoria, robbed of so much. *Rest easy,* she told her sister-in-law, in the silence of her heart. *I'll look after Mary Catherine and Eleanor as long as they need me. I promise you that much.*

The babies were lying on the bed behind her, cooing and kicking, content because they'd just been fed and changed. Looking at them, their lost mother's skates in her hands, Jessica felt a surge of joy so poignant that it was all she could do not to grab up her nieces and hug them with all her might.

June-bug was right; they were precious. Treasures for whom she would go anywhere, do anything.

"I love you," she said to them. And they gurgled happily in response.

The skates might have been made for Jessica, they fit so well, but she was sorely out of practice. She stood, teetering, and flung out her arms for balance, like a high-wire artist performing in a circus. She looked at the babies, who were watching her with expressions of drunken wonder, each exactly matched to the other, although the twins were not identical.

"Suppose I fall through the ice and catch pneumonia and the pair of you are all alone in the world?" she asked.

It wouldn't work as an excuse to stay home from the skating party; even if she did meet with such a dire and dramatic fate, the Parrishes would gladly take her nieces in and raise them with love.

"All right, then," she speculated. "It's sure to be too cold out there for a couple of brand-new babies such as yourselves. Suppose *you* get sick? Why, I simply couldn't bear it."

But the babies would not take ill, her logical side argued. June-bug had told her that careful provision was always made for infants and small children. They would be held and passed around, close by the fire. In the years they'd been holding these community celebrations, not one of the little mites had been lost.

Jessica teetered over and laid a hand to each of the twins' foreheads. Both were satiny cool.

It was settled, then; she'd join the rest of Springwater in heralding what was bound to be a bitterly cold night. She might even enjoy herself, if she could stop worrying long enough.

She removed her skates, put the babies back into their cradle, where they promptly fell asleep, exhausted by a morning spent socializing with June-bug McCaffrey, and made for the kitchen without bothering to put her shoes back on. There, she made a pot of tea.

The brew smelled lovely and rich, and she heated milk to flavor it. She felt afraid of what the future might hold, that was for sure, but there was a certain quiet joy within her, too. For the first time in her life, she was truly on her own. *She* would be the one to make the rules she abided by — not her uncle, not her employer, not even her brother, much as she'd loved him. No, she was going to be independent from here on, and, scary as that was, it made her want to spread her arms and laugh as she had done long, long ago, spinning on the skating pond until the world was a blur of color and shape.

Jacob himself had built the horse-drawn sleigh for just such nights as that one, and it was already full of fresh hay and crowded with laughing people when he drew the team to a halt in front of the newspaper office.

Gage jumped down from the flat bed of the sleigh and marveled at the jittery twitch in the pit of his stomach. Just the prospect of seeing Jessica Barnes again did that to him, and the hell of it was, the reality was bound to affect him even more. He just hoped she didn't slam the door in his face, that was all, with half of Springwater down on the street listening for any word that might pass between the two of them. Trey and Landry were already ribbing him about Miss Barnes anyway, and here he was, letting himself in for more grief.

He hesitated a moment at the foot of the stairs, then bounded up them and knocked hard on the door.

Jessica answered, of course, looking surprised and damnably beautiful, even in her plain brown woolen dress. If it hadn't been for the fact that she was holding a baby in each arm, he would probably have bolted, like some shy kid, rather than risk a rebuff from her, but the twins won him over. He just couldn't walk away from them.

"Put your cloak on," he said, taking both bundles from her with a grace that surprised him as much as it did her, and speaking rapidly, as if that could stop her from changing her mind, saying she wouldn't go. "It's cold out."

She stared at him. "I was planning to walk to the pond," she said.

"Walk? With two babies? Miss Barnes, it's a mile to the springs, and even though the cattle have worn paths through the snow in some places, it's still hard going."

She blinked. He knew she wanted to snatch the babies back and refuse to have anything at all to do with him — it wasn't hard to figure why, given the political differences he'd had with her brother — but he'd be damned if he'd return to that sleigh without her.

He gestured with his head, since his arms were full. "The whole town's waiting down there," he told her impatiently. "So you needn't fear for your virtue."

That brought a blush to her cheeks, a phenomenon he thoroughly and shamelessly enjoyed. She might be a prickly little bluestocking with an icicle for a heart, but she sure made a man want to warm her up and smooth her out.

"Very well," she said, putting on her cloak and snatching up a pair of well-used skates. "I guess I have no choice." She stepped out onto the stair landing, and winter stars caught in her eyes as she looked up at Gage, her expression uncertain, rather than saucy. "I — perhaps we could be civil to each other — just for tonight?"

He wanted to laugh. She might as well have gone on to say that hostilities would resume in the morning, so he shouldn't let himself get too comfortable. "All right," he agreed, with hard-won solemnity. He turned and led the way down the stairs, kicking himself all the way for not coming up with something memorable to say. So much for his reputation as an orator.

He sat close to her aboard the sleigh, ostensibly because he still had charge of one of the babies — June-bug had immediately claimed the other — and was annoyed to find that his heart was beating against his rib cage like a fist. He felt light-headed, as if he were suspended somewhere between the earth and the sky, and he hoped to God it didn't mean what he thought it did.

The last time he'd felt this way, he'd made the mistake of a lifetime, a mistake that had cost him virtually everything he held dear. The sizable trust fund left to him by his maternal grandmother had been — and still was — paltry comfort, compared to the loss of his family, his dreams, and Liza.

Out of the corner of his eye he saw that

Jessica's face was alight; she enjoyed the company of neighbors, if not his company in particular, and knew even then that she would find her heart's home in Springwater. In no time at all, she'd be somebody's wife, deeply cherished.

The idea left a sour scowl in its wake.

Jacob was at the reins, which lay easy in his big hands, and when he glanced back once, his Indian-dark eyes smiled on Gage and Jessica, taking them both in as one, even if his mouth stayed still.

By the time they arrived, both babies had been absorbed into a cluster of chattering, admiring women. Having his arms empty gave Gage the excuse he needed to catch hold of Jessica by her narrow little waist — she didn't weigh much more than a mail sack — and lift her down from the edge of the sleigh. She looked surprised, all right, but he didn't give her a chance to comment. He just took her arm and steered her toward the huge, waiting bonfire, built earlier by Toby and the Kildare boys.

All the while, he wondered what in hell he was doing. Jessica had made it plain that she didn't like him, and he was just asking for trouble by hanging around. He couldn't seem to help it, that was the discouraging thing. It seemed to him that history was repeating itself: he was falling in love with a woman who'd sooner watch him burn than spit to put the flames out.

"This here's Rachel Hargreaves," June-bug said, tugging at Jessica's cloak to get her attention. Jessica turned to see a small, dark-haired woman smiling at her. "Rachel, here's Jessica Barnes. Michael's sister."

There was a brief and respectful silence at the mention of Michael's name, but then, to Jessica's profound relief, the conversation continued.

"And this is Savannah Parrish," June-bug went on, indicating a beautiful woman with red-gold hair. A little girl stood beside her on minuscule skates, clutching her mother's skirts. The child was lovely, pretty as a por-celain doll, and dressed all in rich blue velvet.

This, then, was the woman who wanted to adopt little Mary Catherine and Eleanor. Jessica felt a pang, for it was clear that Mrs. Parrish cherished her own child, and would have been good to the twins, as well. "Hello," Savannah said.

Jessica nodded in response, captivated by the little girl, who displayed her father's dark coloring and her mother's exquisitely formed features.

"I'm four," the child announced.

Jessica smiled. "My goodness," she marveled.

"And I can count."

Savannah bent and kissed her daughter's dark head through her hood of white fur. "Hush, now, Beatrice," she said softly.

Other introductions were made after that, but Jessica soon lost track of who was who. There were so many faces to remember, so many names. And besides, she was almighty nervous, with Mr. Calloway staying so close by the way he was. She was conscious of him in every snippet and fragment of her being.

It was indeed a relief when they finally reached the pond, where the skating party was to take place. A gangly blond boy was already there, sweeping snow off the ice with a straw broom. The light of the fire, some fifty feet away, danced orange over the snow, and wood smoke rolled toward the dark, star-speckled sky, filling the air with a pleasant scent.

Later, Jessica could only account for that night by believing that a passing angel had cast a spell over her. She might have stepped outside the ordinary world for a little while, leaving her sorrows, her doubts, her struggles all behind.

When she sat down on a log to pull on her

skates, Gage appeared and knelt before her in the snow. She knew she should refuse to let him unlace her shoes, run his hands lightly over her ankles, but she couldn't. She was in the grip of some foolish, wonderful magic, and because she was certain it would be brief, she meant to enjoy it.

They skated together, arm in arm, and Jessica even laughed. She felt a part of things — part of Springwater, part of the world and the universe. Part of a couple, however silly that idea would turn out to be, in the harsh light of a winter morning. For that night, she could pretend to be Cinderella on the arm of her prince.

Later, he brought her hot cider, and they engaged in a friendly snowball fight. There was more laughter all around, and Jessica's heart, held to the ground for so long, soared against a dark sky shimmering with stars.

Finally, in the shadow of a tree, one of the few that grew below the foothills, Gage kissed her. She thought she ought to struggle, for the sake of principle, but the plain fact was, she didn't want to. She allowed the kiss, even responded to it, and when it was over, she felt as though east and west, north and south had gotten all mixed up, out of their right places.

She took a handful of snow from a low

branch and tossed it playfully into Gage's face.

He laughed, his arms still resting lightly around her waist. "What makes you such an ornery female?"

"I am *not* an ornery female."

He chuckled. "I see. What are you, then?"

She was stumped for an answer, at least for the moment. The fresh, chilly air — at least, she told herself it was that — made her breathless, and she was feeling slightly intoxicated, the way she had one Christmas Eve, on shipboard, when old Mrs. Covington had persuaded her to have a glass of wine with dinner.

She was starting to remember things, though — that this man had ordered Michael's loans called in. That he wanted the newspaper for himself, was probably only trying to sweet-talk her into selling it. The spell was fading, and she felt an inestimable sorrow, quite different from the loss of her brother and sister-in-law, sweep over her as she stepped back.

"It won't work, Mr. Calloway," she said.

He knew what she was talking about; she could see that in his face. But of course, being a lawyer, and practiced in the various ways and means of turning others to his way of thinking, he tried to keep up the pretense.

"Why do you have to be so suspicious?"

"You destroyed my brother. You persuaded the bank in Choteau to call in his loans. He died because of you and others like you."

Gage stared at her. Apparently he'd thought she hadn't known, and his denial came too late. "I was Michael's friend, whether he knew it or not. One of the best he ever had."

Jessica squared her shoulders and hiked up her chin. The man was stark raving mad; surely he'd seen Michael's editorials. Surely they had exchanged heated words, Gage and her brother.

Well, now the brief idyll was over. It was time she and the babies went home, where they belonged.

Chapter

5

Jessica was up even before the twins the following morning, and after feeding and dressing the pair, she wrapped each one in a wooly blanket and then carried them downstairs, one and then the other, to the newspaper office. They rested comfortably in their separate and well-padded apple crates, which Jessica had scrounged from the shed out back specifically for that purpose. It wouldn't be easy, raising two babies and running the *Gazette* at the same time, but then, she'd never expected anything to be easy. Nor had she been disappointed, at least in that respect.

The office was so cold that a layer of hoary frost covered the floor, and the woodstove was stubborn that morning, filling the whole lower floor with smoke and setting the twins to coughing and wheezing. Half panicked, Jessica threw open the door to the street and tried to shoo the smoke outside by flapping her printer's apron.

Gage Calloway burst in, followed immediately by a woman Jessica had met briefly at the skating party the night before. Her name was Cornucopia, and it suited her well, for she was lushly made, with her shapely figure and dark red hair, the sort men generally took to right away. She ran the general store and, despite Alma's low opinion, seemed to Jessica to be a nice person.

"Good Lord," Gage demanded, "is the place on fire?"

The babies started to wail, and Cornucopia crooned to them, making her way past Gage and Jessica. "I'll take the little darlings over to the store," she said. "They'll be perfectly safe there."

Jessica was grateful for Cornucopia's offer, but she had her hands on her hips as she looked up into Gage's face. It shamed her now, to remember that she'd let him kiss her the night before. Conversely, she wished he'd kissed her again, which only went to show that he was a bad moral influence.

"I do not need your help, Mr. Calloway," she said, suppressing a violent spasm of coughing. Cornucopia went by with one of the babies wailing in its crate, with a murmured promise to return for the other twin in a minute. "Something is wrong with the damper, that's all."

Despite her subtle effort to block his way, he went around her and bent to pick up the other apple crate and, thus, the baby inside. The little traitor immediately stopped crying.

"There, now," he said.

"Put that baby down," Jessica commanded.

Fortunately, Cornucopia returned just then and claimed little Eleanor. "I'll bring them back soon as you've got the place aired out a little," she said, and made a hasty retreat.

Gage looked at Jessica squarely. The air was clearing a little, but it still stung her nose and eyeballs. "I'm not your enemy," he said. "I wasn't your brother's enemy, either. Michael's mind took a strange turn when Victoria died — he thought everyone was against him."

Jessica was mobilized by the mention of Michael. She marched over to the worktable and grasped the page of newsprint her brother had set before his death. She stabbed at the headline with one finger, the one warning that Gage Calloway was out to buy his way straight into the territorial governor's office. "How, then, do you explain this?"

"Ah," he said. "The gospel according to St. Michael."

"Don't you dare impugn my brother's honesty!"

"Your brother was crazy with grief over his wife when he wrote those words. He was about to lose the newspaper —" His voice broke off, and she saw regret in his face.

"Because of you. Because you made the bank in Choteau call in his loans!" Tears scalded her eyes; she told herself it was because of the smoke, and not because she cared for a man and it was hopeless.

He grasped her shoulders. "Listen to me, Jessie," he said. "Michael and I had our differences, there's no denying that. But I sure as hell didn't have anything to do with the bank calling in his note. The fact is, it's in my safe right now."

She felt as though the floor had opened up, as though she were dangling over a dark precipice and would surely fall if Gage merely flexed his fingers. *"What?"*

He let her go, and she didn't fall. She just stood there, stricken to the soul. He thrust a hand through his hair and heaved a great sigh, while the cold Montana wind swept in and chilled them both.

"I hold the note on the newspaper, Jessie," he said at long last. "Legally, it's mine.

Morally — well, that's another question."

This time, her knees did give out. She groped for a chair and sank into it, just in time. Gage closed the door and crossed the room to adjust the stove damper.

He owned the *Gazette*. God in heaven, she had nothing, except for a few hundred dollars tucked away in a St. Louis bank account. Once that small legacy was gone, she and the babies would be destitute.

"Why didn't you tell me? Why did you let me think — ?"

"You had just lost your brother. You were in no condition to hear news like that."

"But you were going to buy something that was already yours. Or were you offering me charity, Mr. Calloway?"

He drew up another chair, with a scraping sound, and sat astride of it, facing her, his arms resting on the high back. His eyes, far from pitying, were snapping with annoyance. "You've got the same kind of stiffnecked pride your brother had," he said evenly. "He couldn't accept help, either. I was his friend, and I believed in him." He paused, sighed. "Michael wanted to be a part of Springwater, but at the same time he held himself apart, just like you're trying to do."

While what he was saying had a certain

ring of truth, it was entirely beside the point, as far as Jessica was concerned. "I do not need your charity."

"Oh, no? Where do you intend to go?"

She was stymied, but only briefly. "I can find work someplace."

"With two babies tagging along? I doubt it."

"What do you propose?"

"That you get married."

"Oh, that's a wonderful solution," Jessica raged. "To whom?"

"To me."

She couldn't believe it — couldn't believe, either, the fiery sensation the suggestion sparked in the deepest regions of her femininity. "You . . . are . . . amazing. Stubborn. *Insane.*" And, for all of it, so damnably appealing.

His face did not soften. She was seeing another side of him now, the ruthless, unbending side that Michael had probably known all too well. "What other choice do you have?"

He'd probably said those same words to her brother. God, what fury he stirred in her — how he intrigued and confused her! And oh how desperately she wished things could be different between them.

"Very well," she heard herself say, from

somewhere in that storm of conflicting emotions. "I'll marry you — I have no real choice, do I? But I promise you, *Mr.* Calloway, that I shall make your life utterly miserable!"

He laughed — actually laughed. "Fair enough," he said. "The nights will compensate more than adequately, I'm sure."

Her mouth fell open. He reached out and closed it by pressing one finger under her chin.

"You expect me to . . . to share your bed?"

"As my wife? Most certainly."

"Then I won't marry you. I'll — I'll —"

"What?" he taunted, but not unkindly. He sounded genuinely curious, damn his hide. "What will you do?"

She bit her lower lip. As an unmarried woman — and a poor one at that — with no family to turn to, her options were severely limited. Furthermore, she had no other offers in hand, and none on the horizon, either. The men of Springwater, it seemed to her, were all married. Even Mr. Brody was courting a woman in Seattle, by telegram, according to Alma.

"I don't love you," she said. Unfortunately, she wasn't at all sure that was true, but she wasn't about to leave herself open to still more trouble by saying so.

He arched an eyebrow. "I don't love you, either."

"Wouldn't it be better if we — if I went on living here, while you lived in your house — just until we get to know each other a little better?"

He immediately shook his head. "I've sold the house," he said. "Some woman back East bought it. She's on her way here right now." He lifted his gaze briefly to the ceiling. "Looks as though we'll have to share the upstairs, just till we've got a place of our own."

She was, for a long moment, tongue-tied. He'd made a case, all right, one she was finding it hard to argue with. Aside from throwing herself and the babies on the mercy of the McCaffreys or one of the other families in Springwater — and she was far too proud to do that — she had no respectable alternatives. She'd heard of women in just such a position becoming prostitutes, and it seemed to her that if she was going to sell herself, she might as well confine her favors to one man. He was not entirely unattractive, after all.

"All right," she said, looking down at her knotted hands. *Forgive me, Michael,* she whispered in her heart. "When?"

He considered the question for a damnably long time. "No hurry," he concluded finally, and got up from his chair. "I'll let you know."

I'll let you know. He meant to leave her wondering, the black-hearted rascal! He probably *enjoyed* seeing her wriggle on the head of a pin.

"You could do worse," Cornucopia said, echoing Alma's sentiments, when Jessica went to collect the babies an hour later. The story of Gage's "proposal," which she'd meant to keep to herself, burst out of her the moment she stepped into the general store. Despite what Alma had said about Cornucopia keeping company with other women's husbands, Jessica liked her. "Heavens to Betsy, if Gage Calloway asked *me* to marry him, I'd be cooking his breakfast and pressing his shirts before you could say 'Here comes the bride.' "

Jessica was completely confused. "You knew, I suppose, about the feud between Mr. Calloway and my brother?"

"I wouldn't call it a feud," Cornucopia said, smiling fondly as one of the babies — Mary Catherine, as it happened — grasped her finger in a fat little baby hand. "Folks can disagree about most everything, it seems to me, and still treat each other decent." She met Jessica's eye across the

111

counter, on which the babies reigned in their apple-crate cradles. "Sit down a spell, there by the stove. It's a cold day, bound to get colder, and you're frazzled. What you need is some hot tea and a little woman talk."

Jessica was too grateful to refuse, even though her pride dictated that she should be able to make her own way without leaning on others for support. She sat down, and enjoyed the delicious warmth emanating from the stove.

"I suppose that old lady told you I'm a man-chaser," Cornucopia said forthrightly, when she returned from what Jessica presumed were the living quarters behind the store, carrying two cups of steaming tea.

Jessica was startled out of her own self-absorption. "Well —"

Cornucopia gave Jessica one of the cups, sat down in the other chair, and waved a hand as if to fan away a bad smell. "Fact is, there was this rancher, over Choteau way. I went to work cooking for him, and we got friendly over the course of a long winter. Trouble was, he didn't mention that he had a wife back East until she showed up one day. What a tongue that woman had! Like to strip the hide off both of us. I lit out right away, I can tell you that, but not before I made that old man give me the wherewithal to start up this store." She sighed and slurped up a mouthful of tea, then swallowed. "Turns out, the missus was a friend of Alma's. Alma never had no use for me from the first."

Astounded, Jessica stared at the other woman. "My goodness," she exclaimed, at long last, as the story unfolded in her mind's eye. She was a while digesting all the images, but when she had, she steered the conversation back onto its original path: the rift between Michael and Gage Calloway. "Why did you say you wouldn't call the animosity between my brother and Mr. Calloway a feud?"

Cornucopia shrugged her ample shoulders. She was truly voluptuous, with large breasts, perfect, glowing skin, and bright green eyes. "There toward the end, you couldn't put a lot of store by the things Michael said. Not that he was lying, mind you. But he was plum beside himself from the time Victoria died."

"He loved her very much."

Cornucopia sighed and nodded. "Yes, he did. But they weren't up to life out here, neither one of them. Some folks just aren't cut out for pioneering."

Privately, Jessica agreed, but out of respect for Michael's memory and all the dreams that had died with him, she didn't say so out loud. "What about Mr. Calloway? What would bring a man like him to a place like Springwater? He doesn't seem to be the pioneer sort, either."

Cornucopia weighed the question for a long time before answering. "From what I gather, he had some family problems back in San Francisco. That's where he hails from, you know. San Francisco. Anyways, he had some sort of falling out with the homefolks and I guess Springwater must have seemed like the other end of the earth to somebody like him. Far as I can tell, he's been happy here." A wistful look came into Cornucopia's eyes, and she fell silent for a few moments. "Lonely, though. Anybody could see that."

Jessica wondered if Cornucopia cared for Gage herself, wondered if he'd ever sought solace in the room or rooms behind the store. She discovered that she hoped not — and fervently — though it shouldn't have mattered.

Cornucopia must have read her mind, for she smiled sadly and said, "Don't you worry, Miss Barnes. I never managed to turn Gage's head even one time, though God knows, I tried. Until you came along, he was so full of whoever it was he left behind that he wouldn't have noticed if I'd stripped off all my clothes and ridden a stagecoach mule down the middle of the street at high noon."

In spite of everything, Jessica couldn't help laughing at the picture that came to her mind. At the same time, she wondered — as if she had any reason at all to care — precisely who Gage had left behind in San Francisco. He'd built that grand house across from the Parrishes' place for her, whoever she was. He probably loved her still.

Jessica put the thought out of her mind, for the moment at least. She had problems enough as it was.

She was alone in the newspaper office half an hour later, having given in to Cornucopia's pleas that she leave the babies at the store, where it was warm, when Gage appeared.

She held her breath, half afraid he'd come to drag her before a preacher, and half afraid that he hadn't. "I brought you some news," he said. "It came in over the wire just a few minutes ago. There's a train missing — one that passes within twenty miles of here. It should have come into Missoula yes-

115

terday afternoon, but there's been no sign of it."

Jessica was horrified. All thought of her own predicaments left her mind. "Have they sent a search party?"

Gage nodded, but his eyes were grim. "No luck. A few of us are going out to ride alongside the track for a ways, just in case."

Jessica glanced at the gaping door, aware for the first time that she was freezing. Hastily, she crossed the room and pushed it shut. The snow, so pretty before, was now coming down in small, slushy flakes, and she could barely see past the windows. "Isn't that dangerous? Going out in this weather, I mean? Cornucopia told me there might be a blizzard coming."

Gage shook his head. "What weather?" he countered good-naturedly. "Miss Barnes, that's just an ordinary winter day out there. When we get hit by a genuine blizzard, there'll be no question in anybody's mind what to call it."

Michael had described some of those storms in his letters, telling how men and cattle froze to death on the range, how whole families smothered in cabins buried past their chimneys in snow. She moved a little closer to the stove and made a concerted effort not to think about such calami-

116

ties — which worked about as well as it ever did.

"Thank you," she said. "For the news, I mean. I'd appreciate any more details you might hear."

He nodded, already on his way to the door. He stopped, one bare hand on the knob. "Miss Barnes?"

"Yes?"

"Try not to burn down the newspaper office while we're gone. If one building goes up, we could lose the whole town, and then we'd all be in as much trouble as those poor souls aboard that missing train." With that, he was gone, giving Jessica no chance to respond. Which, she supposed, was just as well. If it hadn't been for the danger both to the men in the search party and the travelers on the lost train, she would have been relieved. He'd apparently forgotten, for the time being at least, that they were supposed to be getting married.

It was a mercy, that's what it was. So why didn't she feel relieved?

If Mr. Calloway's visit had served no other purpose, it had at least given her something constructive to do. After washing up, Jessica put on her warm cloak and ventured out into the blustery chill. The air was so dry and cold, so crisp that it stung her face, the insides of her nostrils, and even her lungs, and the snow was starting to come down in angry swirls.

A flock of mounted men were milling about down by the Springwater station, and even though they were all wearing long, heavy coats, hats, and mufflers, Jessica spotted Gage right away. He seemed to stand out from the others, as though he'd taken on some extra dimension.

She bent her head against the bitter wind and pushed on until she reached the telegraph office. She would speak directly with the operator concerning the missing train; perhaps she didn't have a lot of experience at running a newspaper, but she knew better than to print pure hearsay.

The telegraph man was a pleasant sort, with ears almost as long as his head and spectacles perched on the tip of his narrow nose. His hair, such as it was, stood up in tufts of salt-and-pepper, and he was quick to smile and tug at the brim of his visor when Jessica came in.

"C. W. Brody," he said by way of introduction. "And you must be Michael's sister."

"Miss Jessica Barnes," she confirmed, politely, but in a businesslike manner. If she was going to be taken seriously as a journalist — however short her career might be

— she must behave like a professional. "I've come to ask about the train."

"Oh, we don't expect to have one runnin' through here much before the turn of the century," Mr. Brody said. "Not straight through Springwater, anyways. There's some that pass by at a distance." He took in her wind-reddened face. "Come and sit down over here by the stove. You look like one of your arms might fall off and clatter around on the floor."

Jessica was disconcerted by that remark, but she recovered right away. Little wonder that she looked cold; she *was* cold. She took a seat within the shimmering haze of heat that surrounded the stove and slipped her cloak back off her shoulders. Then she took a pencil and a pad of paper from her reticule.

"I could brew up some coffee," Mr. Brody suggested. He really was quite dear, and obviously glad of company. No doubt his job was dull most of the time, and lonely into the bargain.

"You wouldn't happen to have tea, would you?" Jessica inquired. She knew that Mr. Calloway shared the building; her gaze had already strayed at least once to the frosted glass door with his name penned across it in gold script.

"I could borrow some from Cornucopia, over at the general store."

She had already imposed on Cornucopia enough as it was, by leaving the babies in her care. "Oh, no," she said hastily, "please. That would be too much trouble."

Mr. Brody, it turned out, was in possession of a great deal more information regarding the vanished passenger train than Jessica would have guessed. He spent a full half-hour giving her the details, right down to the names of the travelers thought to be aboard. One of them, a Miss Olivia Wilcott Darling, who had begun her journey in Chicago, was believed to be headed for Springwater. Mr. Brody lowered his voice and inclined his head slightly toward Jessica when he got to that part. "Gage done sold her his house."

Jessica took thorough notes, but her thoughts were with the men who had ridden out to participate in the search. Or, at least, with *one* of them.

When her professional interview with Mr. Brody ended, she ventured a private inquiry, having guessed that the harmless little man was something of a gossip. "Do you happen to know the precise amount of my late brother's debt to Mr. Calloway?"

Mr. Brody looked stunned, then reluctant. "Why do you ask?"

"I have my reasons," she replied.

He flushed, started to speak, then closed his mouth. Finally he said, "Three hundred and forty-two dollars."

Three hundred and forty-two dollars. Almost the entire amount of Jessica's legacy from Mrs. Covington. But if she had that money in hand, she could pay Mr. Calloway back and throw his marriage proposal in his face right along with it. Furthermore, the newspaper would be hers.

"I should like to send a wire," she said.

The train was half buried under an avalanche of snow when they found it, and the daylight, such as it was, was nearly gone. The horses were completely spent. While Pres and Trey scrambled into the one visible passenger car, which lay on its side in a drift, all of its windows broken out, Jacob, Gage, and Landry set themselves to gathering wood and getting a fire going. If there was anybody left alive inside, they'd be cold as well as hurt — maybe badly.

Gage and Landry were making a sort of lean-to out of fallen branches when they heard a shout echo from within the train. Both of them dropped what they were doing and hurried toward the overturned car, though it was hard, slow going. The wind was rising, and Gage could feel it biting right through his clothes.

Trey scrambled up out of the car through one of the windows, and crouched beside the opening. Just as Gage and Landry reached the scene, Pres handed up a small, inert body from inside — a little boy, Gage realized, no more than four or five years old. Trey took the child gently and passed him down to Landry, who immediately started back toward the lean-to and the fire.

"Here's another one," Trey said, and produced a second boy, this one around seven, and at least half conscious. One of his legs was twisted at an alarming angle, and his short pants and patched jacket were soaked with blood. Soon, Gage too was on his way toward the improvised camp, the lad moaning in his arms.

There was one last passenger — a tall, slender woman of the sort men usually described as handsome. She looked essentially unhurt, though rumpled, shaken up and very, very cold. When Trey lifted her carefully up through the broken train window, she batted at him with her handbag and told him to watch where he put his hands. Five minutes later, the wind was howling like a thousand wolves serenading a full moon, and the bonfire provided scant protection.

"What happened?" Pres asked the woman. He had climbed out of the train and was next to the fire with the rest of them, kneeling beside the boy with the broken leg. He had already set the bone, and now he was applying a splint. The other boy was awake now, but he was pale as death, and his eyes seemed to fill his whole head.

The woman blinked, and Gage realized she was trying to keep from crying. He couldn't say he'd have blamed her if she *had* broken down, after an experience like that. "The train was moving very slowly — mounting a grade, I think. Then we heard a dreadful roaring sound, and — and we were all thrown this way and that —" She paused and put both hands over her face.

Without speaking, Landry pulled a pewter flask from inside his coat and held it out to her. She hesitated for a few moments, then accepted the offering, unscrewed the lid, and poured a good guzzle straight down her throat. Her eyes didn't even water, which was something to behold, because she sure didn't look like the type who could swallow homemade whiskey without so much as a sputter.

"The engineer and the conductor — ?" she began. "Are they — ?"

123

"Dead," Pres said. Sometimes he was about as tactful as a sledgehammer. "You and these boys are the only survivors, I'm afraid. Did you have family on the train?"

She shook her head distractedly, then put a hand to her mouth, scrambled to her feet, and rounded the tree to retch into the snow.

"Couldn't you have broken the news over the space of, say, a paragraph?" Trey demanded of Pres in an irritated hiss.

Pres didn't miss a beat. "What would be the point of that? A fact is a fact. Everybody else on that train was either killed outright or died of exposure."

The smaller boy began to sob. He had a scrap of paper pinned to his coat with the number 18 scrawled on it, along with a name. Gage squinted. "Here now, Tommy," he said. "Everything's going to be all right. You'll see."

"Stop that cryin'," instructed the older boy, through teeth clenched against the pain in his injured leg. "We're alive, ain't we? That makes us lucky, the way I figure things."

Tommy sniffled, making a valiant effort to pull himself together. "But I'm cold, Ben, and I'm hungry, and now we ain't going to be 'dopted."

Gage understood then. The boys were

probably brothers, though not necessarily, who'd been sent west to find homes for themselves. A fair number of these "orphan train" kids ended up working like mules, but a lot of them were taken in by good people and raised as blood kin, too.

The woman returned, looking as ghastly as she surely felt. "We aren't going to spend the *night* out here, are we?" she asked, dabbing at her slender throat with a wadded handkerchief.

Pres gave her a downright unfriendly look, probably worried that she'd raise a fuss and scare those kids even worse. "If we try to go back tonight," he said, "we'll freeze to death."

That was Pres. He knew how to embroider a phrase, all right.

Tommy had moved closer to his brother. "Does that hurt?" he asked, indicating the splint.

Ben took a swat at him but, fortunately, missed. "What do you think?" he snapped.

Gage sighed and leaned back against the trunk of a cottonwood. It was going to be a long night.

"Where did you boys come from?" Pres asked, as he finished up with Ben's leg and then patted him on the shoulder, his way of telling the child he'd been brave.

"Boston," Ben answered. "We was supposed to get adopted." His expression was fierce, even in the firelight. The kid had pride — and plenty of it — though little else, probably. "Tommy's my brother, and we mean to stay together, no matter what. We got to find somebody who wants both of us."

Pres seemed to be in a reflective mood, there for a moment, and he even went so far as to look toward Springwater, which was a good fifteen or twenty miles off. "I think I might know somebody who does," he answered.

Landry elbowed Gage, and out of the corner of his eye, Gage saw that his friend was grinning.

Chapter

6

By the time Gage and the others got back to Springwater, at around noon the next day, roughly half the party was wishing they'd left Miss Olivia Wilcott Darling behind to freeze to death. The other half just hoped she'd hate the place and move on before the first thaw.

With some help from Landry, Pres took the two little boys, Tommy and Ben, to his house. That left Miss Darling to deal with. It was ironic as hell, in Gage's considered opinion, her having a name like that, and more ironic still that she'd turned out to be the very woman who'd bought his house, sight unseen. She meant to stay at the Springwater station until she'd rested up enough to take possession of the place, which she intended to turn into a rooming house — so it fell to Trey to get her to June-bug before somebody lost their head and strangled her.

Gage was numb with cold and too tired to think. If he'd been a drinking man, he would have taken a shot of whiskey; as it was, he was considering taking up the habit. He left his worn-out horse tethered to the hitching rail out in front of the telegraph office and went inside, intending to stand by the stove for a while before moving on to his cubbyhole in the back and collapsing onto the too-short horsehair settee he usually reserved for clients with a tendency to overstay their welcome. He didn't expect to wake up for the better part of a week.

Nor did he expect to encounter Miss Jessica Barnes — his intended, he recalled with some surprise — when he stepped over the threshold. He already thought of her as "Jessie," though he was prudent about using the nickname, her being somewhat of a prickly type.

She was standing at the telegraph counter with a message in both hands, and it looked as though she might tear the thing right in two, she was holding it so tightly.

"Bad news?" he asked. Seeing her was better than whiskey.

She looked up at him, blinked — evidently she'd been so absorbed that she hadn't heard the door open — and shoved the telegram into the pocket of her cloak.

"Nothing that need concern you," she said, for all the world as if she hadn't agreed to be his wife just the day before. "Did you find the train?"

He thrust out a long sigh, hung up his hat, and shrugged out of his sodden coat. There was no sign of C.W., which was just as well, because he wasn't up to being questioned by him, too. "We found it. Most everybody was killed outright."

Jessica went pale, and for a moment he thought he ought to reach out and steady her, but she rallied quickly. "Most everybody?" she asked.

"A woman survived, and two little boys. Twenty others weren't so lucky."

She looked past him, through the heavy glass in the door. "You just left them all out there?"

He gave her a level look before moving around her, drawn to the welcoming warmth of the stove. "No. A couple of railroad agents showed up around dawn, with a hired posse. They're taking the bodies to Missoula."

She swallowed. "That's dreadful. So many people, gone."

At least she wasn't scribbling down details, like a lot of reporters might have done. He nodded, and for the first time the true extent of the tragedy came home to him — maybe he'd been holding it at bay all this time. Now, suddenly, he felt like breaking things. Raging against the impervious forces of life and death, and no matter that it would be futile. He might feel better for doing it.

Jessica ran the tip of her tongue over her lips — it was an innocent gesture, he was sure — but it set something rusty grinding into motion within him, something long-still and silent. Until he'd caught sight of her for the first time, anyway.

"I spoke with Mr. Brody yesterday," she said.

"I wish I could have been here," he replied.

She gave him a look fit to strip paint but, perhaps out of respect for the recently dead, she did not lose her temper. He was disappointed, given that it would have been a pleasant distraction to watch. She was a passionate woman, though she did not seem to realize it. Yet.

"He told me how much Michael owed you."

Gage couldn't work up anything more than mild irritation; he was just too damn tired. Maybe when he'd rested up, he would get C.W. by his skinny, wattled neck and squeeze till he turned blue, but appealing as the prospect was, it would have to wait. It was all he could do not to keep from stretching out on the floor, right there by the stove, and going to sleep. "Did he, now?" he asked. He had hoped Jessica would drop the subject but, of course, she didn't.

"I've wired St. Louis for my personal funds. They are sending the money to a bank in Choteau. All I have to do is pick it up."

"In case you haven't noticed, Miss Barnes, there is a blizzard brewing out there." He thrust a hand through his hair. Maybe he'd have that whiskey after all. "Besides that, it's too late. The documents have already been transferred." He was being ornery and he knew it, but he was too exhausted to mind his manners.

She went paler still. "If you have any decency in you, Mr. Calloway, you will accept full payment and surrender control of the *Gazette* immediately. I, after all, am the rightful owner."

"I am the rightful owner," he pointed out.

She looked, for a moment, as though she would haul off and slap him. "Are you going to insist that we go through with this farce of a marriage?"

131

He smiled. "A deal's a deal," he reminded her.

She turned on one heel and stormed out.

He should have gone after her, should have apologized, should have said of course he'd give back the newspaper and let her out of their agreement, but he simply didn't have the stamina. It would all have to wait.

He slept for two solid days.

The weather was clear the morning he came around, and cold as a coal-digger's ass, but everybody knew there was more snow coming. You could smell it, feel it in the air.

C.W. greeted him somewhat sheepishly when Gage came out of the office in search of hot coffee. "Good to see you up and around, Gage," he said, and looked away quickly.

Gage went to the stove, poured a mug full of sludge from the coffeepot, and took a bracing sip. It was so rank he almost spit it out, but his early training in the social graces wouldn't allow him to do so. "You've got a big mouth, C.W.," he said.

C.W.'s ears turned red. "I don't know what you're talking about."

"Like hell you don't," Gage replied, flinging the miserable coffee into the fire, where it sizzled and hissed. "You told Jessica

Barnes how much her brother owed me."

C.W. swallowed.

"Didn't you?" Gage persisted.

The other man gulped, then nodded. "It was out of my mouth before I knew it, Gage. She just looked at me with those eyes of hers and I turned right into an idiot." Settled at his table, C.W. began tapping out a message. "I don't suppose it'll help much, but I'm sorry."

Gage shoved a hand through his hair. He needed a bath, a shave, fresh clothes, and a heaping plate of June-bug McCaffrey's cooking, in that order. He'd do his thinking afterward.

Half an hour later, he was sitting in the McCaffreys' tin washtub, scrubbed clean, and the smell of good Southern food filled the air. Once he'd eaten, he'd go to Jessica and tell her he hadn't meant what he said about forcing her to marry him. Indeed, he might even tell her that he thought about her a lot and that he had strong feelings for her, and those were facts he'd only recently admitted to himself.

Jessica came out of the bank in Choteau, her life savings tucked carefully into her handbag, and looked right and left. Just down the street, the Springwater stage was

133

waiting. She didn't recognize the driver, but no matter. She had the money to pay Gage, and she needed to get back to the babies and the *Gazette* as soon as possible. She had a complete issue typeset and ready to print, and as soon as she'd fetched the twins back from the general store, where Cornucopia was looking after them, she meant to go to press.

She glanced up at the sky. It was a clear, icy blue, but there were gray clouds gathering on the horizon. Just looking at them made her shiver.

She went to the coach, where the driver was already loading her battered satchel into the boot. "Ma'am," he said, and touched the brim of his hat. "You travelin' out Springwater way?"

"Yes," she nodded, politely, but distantly. "Will the coach be leaving on time?"

"Yes, ma'am," he said, and tugged at his hat again. "I'm Jack Arthur, and I'll be filling in for Guffy today. He's down with a touch of the ague." Turning his head, he assessed the sky, just as Jessica had done moments before. "We've got a storm comin' in, ma'am," he said, when he met her gaze again. "I don't know as you oughtn't to stay right here in Choteau. It might be rough going out there."

Jessica felt a shiver climb her spine, but she shook her head. She had two children waiting for her, and a newspaper to run. Besides that, she couldn't afford to spend another night at the roominghouse, let alone several. Paying back Gage Calloway was going to take most of the money she had. "I'd rather go home," she said.

Arthur nodded. "Yes, ma'am," he said and, with one more wary glance at the sky, helped her aboard the coach. Soon they were traveling toward Springwater, moving at a brisk pace, and if the inside of the stage was a little cold, well, Jessica wasn't about to complain. She just pulled her cloak around her a little more tightly and sat back on the hard, uncomfortable seat, resigned to a long, difficult trip.

During the ride she thought of the train wreck. It seemed as vivid in her mind as if she'd actually witnessed it, complete with all its horrors. She'd written a long and thoughtful article before leaving Springwater, having gotten by wire from the railroad's head office in Missoula a list of those killed, and the story, along with a few minor items of strictly local interest, would make up her first issue of the *Gazette*.

In point of fact, next week's issue was already taking shape in her mind. She would print the first installment of the serial Emma Hargreaves was writing under a pen name, along with notice of the quilting bee in the home of Mrs. Trey Hargreaves the last week of the month, and June-bug McCaffrey's recipe for sweet potato pie. In a town like Springwater, you had to make do with whatever news you could scrape up.

Jessica felt a wrench when she thought of the babies. They'd looked like little golden-haired cherubs, lying there in their padded apple boxes on the counter at the general store, their lashes brushing their round little cheeks. At some point, she had come to love them fiercely, and she knew it was forever. Raising them would not be easy, but then, worthwhile pursuits seldom were.

Why, the mere thought of those children renewed her determination to overcome every obstacle, every setback, every heart-break. She *would* build a life, for the babies and for herself. One thing was for sure: she didn't need Gage Calloway.

So why, she wondered, did this triumph lose a little of its glow when her mind turned, inevitably, to him? It was almost as if she were *disappointed,* which was plain silly.

Back at the Springwater station, June-bug McCaffrey had bid her farewell with a worried look and a hug. "I'm not sure it's a good idea for you to take to the road when the weather's like this," the older woman had fretted. "Why, yesterday when Guffy came through, it took us an hour just to thaw him out!"

Jessica wanted to pour her heart out to June-bug, tell her all her most secret hopes and dreams. Maybe she'd be able to make sense out of the tangle of feelings that had their beginning in Gage Calloway.

A frigid wind rattled the blind covering the stagecoach window, and Jessica moved it aside to peer out. Snow was coming down so hard that she could barely see, and she wondered, with sudden and piercing fear, how the driver could keep the rig on the road in such weather.

For the first time, she wished she hadn't been the only passenger traveling to Springwater that day. She would have taken some consolation from having another soul to talk with.

The disaster struck suddenly, as disasters generally do — before Jessica even had time to wonder what was happening, she'd been flung against the far wall of the stage, and with enough force to leave her dazed and aching all over. The wind was howling so loudly that she couldn't hear the horses or the driver. Snow blew through the broken door of the stage, stinging like a shower of sparks, and she realized with a sick feeling that the rig was half overturned. Struggling to the door and peering out, she caught a glimpse of one spinning wheel before the storm swallowed up even that.

She shrank, shivering, back into the questionable shelter of the coach.

Perhaps it was minutes later, perhaps it was hours, but the driver appeared in the chasm, his face bloodied, his hat gone. "I'll try to make it to the station and fetch back some help," he shouted. "You'd best stay here!"

Jessica wanted to go with him, wanted more than anything in the world not to be left in that bleak place, but she could see the sense in his argument, even then. The coach provided at least some shelter, inadequate though it was, and venturing out into that storm, even on horseback, was a monumental risk.

"What about the mules?" she hollered back.

"I let 'em go, except for old Squirrely, him bein' the best of the lot!" yelled the driver. "Leastways they've got half a chance that way, sorry critters that they are. You stay right here, now! You go wanderin' off somewheres, and you'll be a goner for sure!"

Jessica nodded, too cold and too shaken to carry on such a demanding conversation, and settled back to wait.

"She'll stay in Choteau," Jacob said quietly, aligning the checker pieces for another game while Gage paced the length of the hearth, about as agitated as he'd ever been over anything. "Miss Barnes might be headstrong, but she ain't stupid."

Gage went to the nearest window and glared out, watching as the snowflakes came down thicker and faster. Fifteen inches had fallen since morning, by his measurements. "No," he agreed. "She isn't stupid. But she'll try to come back because of the babies and that damned newspaper. Damn it, if Guffy decides to make today's run, she'll be aboard the stage for sure!"

"Maybe Guffy will stay in town," Jacob reflected, but he was beginning to sound uncertain.

"In the five years I've lived in this town," Gage argued, "I've never known that Irishman to miss a day's work. I'm telling you, Jacob, the two of them are going to freeze to death out there somewhere, right along with eight of your mules."

Jacob sighed, lifted the checkerboard off the table, and let the pieces slide back into their box. "And you figure the smart thing to do would be to ride out there and freeze to death with them."

Gage started pacing again. "I'll go crazy if I don't make sure she's — they're all right."

Jacob replied with one of those rare smiles of his. "So you've finally found her, have you? I don't mind sayin', it's about time. June-bug and I, we were beginnin' to despair of you."

"What the devil are you talking about?" Gage demanded, even though he knew. God help him, he knew.

"You're in love with the gal," Jacob said. "Soon as I heard you'd milked a cow for her, right in front of God and everybody, I suspected as much."

Gage muttered a swear word. The hell of it was, Jacob was right. He just hadn't been ready to admit it aloud until now.

"Isn't this what you've been wantin'? Somebody to care about? Somebody to go home to of a night?"

Gage's mind had left Springwater ahead of him, and taken his heart right along with it, and he was scrabbling to catch up. "I don't have time to talk about this," he said, heading for the door. "I've got to find her."

He slammed out the door and strode

through the dense snowfall toward the barn. Then he remembered his coat, and went back to fetch it.

"Don't you say one damn word," he warned when Jacob shook his head.

Fifteen minutes later, he set out to find the Springwater stage. His horse was opposed to the idea, and they had hard words before the matter was settled to Gage's satisfaction.

A few times, he wasn't sure of his direction, and after an hour he was wearing a bandanna over his face like a bandit, in hopes that he wouldn't lose his nose to frostbite. As he rode, he wondered how it was possible for a man to come to care so deeply for a woman that he'd risk his life for her — not to mention a perfectly good horse — in just a couple of days' time. After wrestling with the question for a while longer, he decided it didn't matter how it happened, or why. It was so, and that was that, and he'd just have to figure a way to deal with the situation.

He doubted that Miss Barnes even *liked* him, though he'd felt a charge pass between them on more than one occasion, and he knew she'd felt it too; even so, she probably would have died before she confessed to bearing him any tender sentiments.

He could no longer tell whether it was night or day when at long last he came upon the stagecoach, a mile this side of Willow Creek and lying on its side. Somebody had unhitched the mules, and they'd headed for the timber, but there was no sign of either O'Hagan or Miss Jessica Barnes.

For the first time since he was eight years old and standing at the foot of his mother's deathbed, Gage Calloway uttered a prayer. He didn't figure even God could hear it, though, the way the wind was screaming, driving snow into his flesh like little spikes. Half blinded, he urged the balking horse forward. The new snow was soft, but the layer beneath was sharp enough to cut flesh.

Then he saw her. She looked out the stage window, her face like a flicker of light in the white gloom, and called out to him. Fearing that he was seeing her ghost, he spurred the anxious horse in a vain effort to get it to move faster.

Finally, after a long struggle with the forces of an angry wind, he reached the side of the coach, bent, and pulled the door open. Jessica crawled and scrambled up to him, flinging her arms around his neck. She was soaked to the skin.

"Where's Guffy?" he yelled, in an effort to be heard over the storm.

"Guffy stayed in town — the other driver went for help —"

Gage turned the horse back toward the station, and they were halfway up a high drift when the animal slipped, shrieking in terror, and flung them both off, one in one direction, one in the other.

Unhurt, the horse scrabbled the rest of the way up the slope and ran, reins dangling, making damn good time considering that the snow was knee-deep by then. Gage made a mental note to enter that gelding in a race, should he live to round it up again.

He hurried back down the bank and hauled Jessica out of the snow with one powerful wrench of his arm. If she'd been in danger before, she was far beyond that point now, soaked to the skin as she was, and covered in snow. He had to find shelter within a matter of minutes, or she would die for certain.

He lifted her into his arms and followed his instincts through the trees, for he was too cold by then to think. He had one aim and one aim only: to keep her alive. If he failed, his own life wouldn't be worth a damn.

He fell to his knees, once, twice, a third time. And each time, he got up again, impelled by a force no preacher had ever told him about. His chest burned, his arms and legs were numb, but she was there, huddled against his chest, and he could feel the beat of her heart. It was enough to keep them both going.

"Don't you dare die, do you hear me?" Gage gasped, close to her ear.

He was all but walking on his knees when the corner of the mine shack came into view, and at first he thought his eyes were fooling him. He'd read about things like this happening to people lost in storms — sometimes they saw visions and thought they were safe, only to succumb a few paces further on.

The door gave when he put his shoulder to it, and he heard the creak of ancient hinges, even over the incessant shrieking of the wind. The whole place swayed when he carried Jessica over the threshold and, for a moment, he just stood there, braced to take the weight of the roof, along with about two feet of accumulated snow and ice.

The walls held, by some miracle. Slowly, awkwardly as a man moving through some thick substance, Gage laid Jessica down on the board floor and forced the door closed. There was next to no light in the place, but once his eyes adjusted, he could see that the structure was about eight by eight.

Lying at his feet, Jessica groaned, and his mind, befuddled by the cold, sent a sluggish message to his hands and legs. After searching the cabin, he found nothing at all to wrap her in, though there were a few twigs and floorboards that could be used to get a fire going. Hastily, he flung his hat aside, then peeled off his coat and started to put it around Jessica.

Another communication sank in. She couldn't stay in these wet clothes.

He stripped her, something he'd imagined doing once or twice, but in his imagination the circumstances had been different. Her bare skin was blue-white, and he bound her up in the coat, then set himself to rubbing her hands and feet, trying to get the circulation going again.

She whimpered. "That . . . hurts."

"Good," he said. "You're alive."

"Where . . . ?"

"Never mind where we are. Hell, I don't even know. Right now, Jessie, I want you to think about those babies, and how much they need you. I want you to think about the newspaper, and — and —" He'd been about to say *me*.

Her eyelashes fluttered against her blue-and-red blotched cheeks. Good God, even frozen half to death, she was beautiful. "And — what?"

"Never mind."

She opened her eyes and looked right through to his soul, or so it seemed to him then, in those frantic moments. "You . . . came looking for me. In this storm."

"Damn good thing, too," he said, shivering now as his flesh began to thaw. In many ways, that was the most miserable part, the painful process of getting warm again. "You'd be dead if it wasn't for me."

Unbelievably, she smiled. "Why? Why would you take such a chance?"

"Why the devil do you think?" he snapped. His teeth were chattering by then, and he was in no mood to chat. "Because I love you, that's why!"

She stared at him. "You do?"

"I said it once, woman. I'm not going to say it again. Not here, not now!"

She laughed, actually *laughed*, with both of them right there on the verge of their just rewards. "You have to be the stubbornest man in the world," she said. Then, with a smile on her lips, she closed her eyes and drifted off someplace just beyond Gage's reach.

Chapter

7

She dreamed they were back out in the storm. She had never been so cold; her clothes clung to her, sodden with melted snow, and she had long since lost all sensation in her limbs. She knew Gage, who was carrying her close against his chest, believed her to be unconscious, but she could not summon the stamina to let him know she was awake.

In those agonizing minutes, when she knew that she was close — so very close — to death, she wanted to live with a passion more ferocious than any she had ever felt before. She wanted to live for the twins, for this impossible man who would not let her die, for herself. For the first time ever, she was centered squarely within herself, sure of who she was and whom she might become, given the chance.

She had the strength for only a scrap of a

prayer, but it shone from the innermost regions of her heart like a beacon, and she was sure God and all his angels could see it. *Please* . . .

She closed her eyes then, and found that she was lying in a dark place. She was warm, though, and she could have sworn that Gage had his arms around her, that he was holding her close against him, as if he feared to let her go.

The cold jabbed Gage awake like a sharp stick; he sat up, careful not to disturb Jessie, and looked around. That old shack seemed flimsy enough to fall over at any second, but it was one hell of a lot better than nothing.

The fire was nearly out; he'd have to get dressed and find more wood. Drawing in a hissing breath, he left the cocoon he'd shared with Jessie and dragged on his pants and shirt, then his boots. The wind was still screaming fit to deafen anybody, but Jessie didn't so much as stir.

Suddenly fearful, he crouched and laid the backs of his fingers to the pulse at the base of her throat. A long sigh escaped him. Her heartbeat was strong and steady. For the moment, nothing else mattered much.

Once again he assessed their surroundings. It was almost as cold inside as out, and the place smelled of mice and other such critters, but there were walls and a roof, and a rusty little woodstove stood in one corner, draped in shadows and cobwebs. He'd started a fire in it — how long ago? — before lying down with Jessie.

Moving as quickly as his still-stiff limbs would allow, Gage scrounged in the darkness for whatever scraps of firewood he might be able to find. In the end, he broke up a crate and stuffed that into the belly of the stove, along with a collection of miscellaneous debris. A blaze caught, spawned by the dying embers of the first fire.

After adjusting the damper on the chimney pipe — he could only hope there were no birds or mice nesting along its twisted length — he set to smashing the remaining furniture, which consisted of one broken chair and a bedstead. Then, when the chill was beginning to subside a little, he lay down beside Jessie again, wrapping the coat around both of them.

He was only human. He enjoyed it a little.

Damn. She was naked. He felt like a kid, peering through a hole in the bathhouse wall. He could feel her softness right through the legs of his trousers and the longjohns beneath.

He positioned her as close to him as he

dared, reminded himself that he was a gentleman, and closed his eyes. Try as he might, he couldn't sleep. He just lay still, in a sort of dull-headed haze, listening to the wind and breathing in the scent of Jessie's hair. Even there, in that filthy, tumbledown shack, she smelled good.

Hours had passed, by his calculation, when he couldn't stand it anymore. She felt too cold, too still. "Jessie?" He patted her cheeks. "Hey, Jessie . . . wake up, will you?"

"I'm . . . awake," she said, in a sort of languid whisper. "Where . . . ?"

"We're in a shack," he reminded her. "Remember, I told you before. Just about the time we were both done for, here it was, like it was waiting for us." He glanced warily up at the rafters, which moaned with every snow-laden gust of wind. There was no telling how long it would be before it gave way, but he didn't plan on mentioning that. "Jacob and June-bug must be praying again."

She smiled, and the plain courage of that twisted something in Gage's heart.

"If anybody's praying for us," she said weakly, "I hope it's them." She sighed, and her lashes, thick and golden brown, fluttered against her cheeks.

"Stay awake, Jessie," he commanded and, still kneeling beside her, he drew her up onto his thighs and held her like a child. In a few minutes, he'd start walking her around the cabin in hopes of getting her blood flowing, but he didn't want to push her too hard. "Did the driver say where he was going?"

She frowned, as though it was an effort to remember. Her expression was dreamlike, and Gage feared that she might be losing ground again. They were by no means out of the woods.

He got to his feet, hauling her with him, and made her walk. "Jessie," he said. "Listen to me. I know you want to sleep, but that's the worst thing you could do right now. I shouldn't have let you close your eyes. You've got to keep moving."

"But . . . I'm so numb. . . ."

"Yes," he agreed. "When things start hurting, then you can lie down. Now, what did he say?"

She thought long and hard. "Who?" she asked, after all that effort.

At least she'd gotten that far. "Did he try to make it to Springwater? Jessie, I'm talking about the driver. Was he headed for town?"

She nodded, but not until they'd been around the inside of the cabin half a dozen times. "He said I'd be safer where I was . . ."

Gage hoped the poor bastard *had* succeeded in reaching the station, because he'd almost certainly be dead of exposure by now if he hadn't. The coach had broken down only about two miles from the station, and in good weather a man could walk the distance without undue wear on the soles of his boots. In a blizzard, it was another matter; there were a hundred ways to get lost, even if you knew the terrain, the way the relief driver surely did. He hoped the McCaffreys would offer up a few prayers for him, too.

"I have to lie down now," Jessica said.

"Not yet," Gage replied.

"I suppose we'll have to spend the night here."

He sighed. "We'll be lucky if we get out of this place in a week, Jessie."

She looked up at him with wide eyes. "A *week?* I'll be ruined!"

"You'll be *dead*, if you go out there before the weather clears."

"What will we do for food? For firewood?"

Her brain was thawing out; he supposed that was a good sign, though pretty soon her fingers and toes would probably start paining her pretty seriously. "You let me worry about the practical things, and just think about getting warm, all right?"

"But you must be cold, too. . . ."

He had been, but Jessica's presence had worked wonders. His skin stung and his bones ached, but except for those things, he felt about normal. "I'm fine," he said. "I could do with some whiskey, though."

She laughed, and if he'd had any doubts that he loved her, they faded to nothing right then. He wished he could tell her again, now that he was sure she'd hear, but he just couldn't bring himself to take the risk. If she rejected him, nothing else in his life was going to matter for a long, long time.

And so they walked, and walked, and walked some more. Finally, when he was sure it was safe to let her rest, he allowed her to lie down again, and she tumbled immediately into a deep and healing sleep. He ferreted around the dingy cabin and found some old gunnysacks to place over her in lieu of blankets, and listened with increasing dread to the shriek of the wind. Every new gust seemed to rattle the whole place, and a couple of times he really thought it was going to collapse into a heap, burying them both in snow, rafters, and rotten shakes. Worse, they were running low on firewood.

He didn't have much choice in the matter; they could freeze to death, or he could go out in the storm and see what he could scare up to stuff into the stove. As for food, well, they'd just have to do without that, because no sensible rabbit or deer was going to be out in weather like that, and the bears were all hibernating.

After making sure Jessica was covered as well as possible, he drew a deep breath, opened the door, and stepped over the threshold. The cold hit him with an impact that stole his breath and nearly blew him right back inside. He ducked his head and kept going.

Jessica was alone — she knew that before she even opened her eyes — and an awful sense of fear rose within her as she sat bolt upright. It was then that she realized she was covered in empty potato sacks and wearing Gage's long coat — with nothing underneath. She vaguely remembered him removing her wet clothes, but at the time she hadn't cared. Even now it didn't bother her half as much as knowing he was outside somewhere in that screaming storm, with nothing to protect him from the cold.

She sat up and tossed the potato sacks distastefully aside, only to pull them over her again when she felt the chill. The fire in the little stove was almost out, and she could see her breath. How long had Gage been gone? Suppose he was lost out there somewhere, wandering around in circles, as winter travelers were known to do?

She opened the stove door and prodded the embers inside with a stick she'd found lying on the floor. Then, awkwardly, she got up, holding the coat and the gunnysacks around her in a vain effort to keep warm, and looked about for a window. There was none. The small amount of daylight entering the cabin was coming in through a wide crack in one of the walls.

More for something to do than because she thought it would do any real good, she hunted around until she found more scraps of burlap. She wadded them into a ball and stuffed them into the gap, and when she did, the whole structure trembled and gave a long, low groan of protest. A shower of dust fell from the rafters.

Jessica gasped and squeezed her eyes shut, inwardly bracing herself, but by some miracle, the roof and walls held. Jacob and June-bug *must* be praying, she thought. It couldn't be her pitiful little "please" that was keeping that building up.

She was just beginning to panic again when the door opened and Gage came in. He looked like a snowman come to life, with his hair and eyebrows frosted and his clothes coated with gleaming white, but he was carrying an armload of wood.

Jessica pushed the door shut behind him, alarmed by the way he moved as he labored across the small room and dropped the precious branches and chunks of bark on the floor. He was stiff and slow as he opened the stove and began shoving things inside.

"Gage Calloway," she said, more out of fear than conviction, "you're a damn fool. Why, look at you — you're covered in ice from head to foot!"

He didn't say anything; he just knelt there, in front of that fire, willing it to burn. Finally the blaze caught, and Jessica could not be sure whether it was the warmth that drew her, or Gage himself. She got down on the floor next to him and began peeling off his clothes, just as he'd done with hers earlier, when they'd first found shelter, and he didn't fight her. She removed his shirt first, then his boots, then his trousers and longjohns. He was trembling, and his skin was an alarming shade of blue.

Instinct caused her to open the coat and enclose him inside it with her, and for a while, they shivered together. It would have been a mercy if she hadn't been so conscious of his nakedness, but she was. Indeed, she felt the contact with him in every pore and follicle. His member, which she had not been able to avoid glimpsing in the process of undressing him, took on a life of its own and pressed itself into the soft flesh of her belly, hard and growing harder with every passing moment.

"Sorry," he said. His teeth were chattering.

"Shhh," she replied, and they lay down together and slept, entwined.

When Jessica awakened again, the room was warmer, and Gage had gotten up and put his clothes back on. She was glad he couldn't know that she missed the feel of him, the strength and substance of him, pressed against her. She was careful not to look at him until the heat in her cheeks had subsided a little, even though the cabin was dark, but for the light of a single tallow candle.

"It's warm," she said.

"I tore up some of the floorboards," he replied. "And I found a jug of corn liquor underneath. Want some? I'm afraid it's the closest thing to supper we're going to get."

Jessica seldom took spirits, but this was surely a time for exceptions. She nodded, and he brought her the jug, held it to her lips, and tilted it so that she could take a sip.

It was like drinking kerosene, and she sputtered and coughed so violently that Gage felt called upon to slap her on the back, but the moonshine produced a spill of fiery warmth as it flooded down her throat and burned its way to her stomach.

"More?" he asked.

She shook her head and wiped her mouth with the back of one hand. "Let me recover for a little while first," she croaked.

He laughed and took an enormous swallow, hooking one finger through the small handle and supporting the jug on the side of his elbow and upper forearm.

She peered at him in the dim light. "What are we going to do?"

He considered awhile, took another swig of whiskey, and answered, "Wait. This storm has got to let up sometime, and when it does, folks will be out looking for us."

"We could get awfully cold and hungry before that happens," she said sensibly.

He set the jug aside and cupped her face with one hand. "They'll find us, Jessie," he promised.

Jessica didn't protest the familiar form of address; in fact, she rather liked it. She wondered if she'd ever be able to admit, outside her own heart and mind, that she loved this man. That she never wanted to be with anybody but him, in spite of everything.

He leaned his head down then and kissed her, softly at first, and then with a heat that made parts of her ache. When the tip of his tongue brushed lightly across her lips, she opened to him, and the sensations that followed left her speechless.

"Jessie," he said, when it was over, and she was still trying to recover her equilibrium. "I love you. I know I must sound like a damn fool, saying a thing like that when we've only been acquainted a few days — and spent most of that time arguing — but it's true."

She stared at him. Maybe it was shock that made her think she'd heard him say he loved her. Maybe it was the cold, or she was coming down with some sort of fever.

"Jessie," he prompted.

"Did you actually say — ?"

"I said I love you," he told her clearly.

Tears filled her eyes. She'd almost given up hope of hearing those words, certainly had never expected to hear them from this particular man, but he'd said them all right, and apparently, he meant them. "I — I love you, too," she said, and just those simple, hesitant words took all the bravery she could summon up. Far more than surviving the storm had required, or traveling west alone, or taking on the raising of twins and the publication of the *Gazette.*

"Marry me," he said.

She swallowed. This proposal was distinctly different from the last one, which had been a mockery. "I have the babies to think of, and the newspaper. And then there are Michael's debts."

"We'll raise the babies together," he said. "With a few of our own, of course. As for the rest, we'll work it out."

She shook her head. "No," she said. "We have to come to an understanding right now. I know Michael owed money to a lot of other people, not just in Springwater, but in Choteau, too. I won't let you take on my brother's debts, Gage, if that's what you're planning on doing. And if I'm going to reimburse the people he borrowed from, I have to make the newspaper pay."

"But you'll marry me? If I agree to your terms, I mean?"

She felt reckless and wild, as though she were careening down a snowy mountainside on a runaway toboggan, and she'd never been happier. "Yes," she said, and he kissed her again.

Come morning, the world was still and the sun shone on miles of snow with a blinding brightness. Jessica and Gage had slept in each other's arms through the night, but both of them had been fully dressed, their clothes having dried, and they had not gone beyond the kissing stage. Jessica might have given in, had he tried to persuade her, for he had awakened things within her that were as elemental as weather, but he'd said they ought to wait until Jacob had said the proper words over them, and she'd agreed.

Both of them had suffered for the sacrifice.

"Shut the door," Gage grumbled, when he awakened and saw Jessica standing on the threshold, one hand shading her eyes, gazing out on the landscape in a state of pure wonder.

Just as she was doing so, they heard a shout from somewhere in the near distance, and Gage nearly knocked her over getting outside.

"Over here!" he yelled, cupping his hands to his mouth.

Snow slid off the roof with an angry, scraping roar, loosed by the sound, and the little shack wobbled, but held. Jessica peered around Gage's broad shoulder, still bundled in his coat, and saw two men come over the nearest drift, wearing snowshoes. Each of them carried another pair strapped to his back.

"I told you they'd find us," Gage said.

Jessica raised her eyes heavenward and offered another silent prayer. *Thank you.*

The men were Trey Hargreaves and Landry Kildare, and they'd brought food as well as blankets and extra snowshoes. When they produced cold biscuits and jerked venison from their packs, both Gage and Jessica ate ravenously.

The trek back to Springwater was long and difficult, and there were times when Jessica thought for sure she would drop to her knees in the hard-crusted snow, never to rise again, but her pride kept her going. If the men could prevail against the elements, so could she. After all, they were all made of the same stuff — blood, bones, breath, and flesh — it was just arranged a little differently in her case.

All during the long journey, she waited for Gage to mention that he and Jessica meant to be married, but the conversation revolved around other things. Jack Arthur had gotten to the stagecoach station safely, though he'd nearly lost some toes and fingers in the effort, and he'd been the one to suggest that they look for Gage and Jessica at the cabin. Jacob had known the prospector who'd settled the place, and everyone had agreed that if indeed the two had found sanction from the weather, that had to be where they were.

It went without saying, of course, that if they *hadn't* gotten in out of the cold, they would surely have perished within a few hours.

Their reception in Springwater raised Jessica's flagging spirits a little — had she only *imagined* Gage telling her he loved her, proposing marriage, holding her throughout the night in an innocent embrace that had, all the same, left her branded as his, forever and ever?

June-bug McCaffrey threw a blanket around Jessica the instant she stepped over the threshold of the Springwater station, guided her to a chair next to the fire, *tsk-tsk*ing all the while, and thrust a cup of hot lemon juice and honey, laced with something a bit stronger, into her hands. She went right on fussing and fetching, murmuring prayers of gratitude, sounding as distractedly joyous as a mother hen who has just rounded up a pair of stray chicks.

Gage was welcomed, too, of course, but in a different way. Jacob brought out his special cider, and he and the other men sat around one of the long trestle tables, listening as the wanderer recounted his harrowing adventures. Jessica listened carefully with one ear, and there was not a word about the plans they had made together.

Had he forgotten? Changed his mind?

"I'd best get home," she said finally, when she felt she could trust her legs to carry her as far as the newspaper office. She made to lift herself out of that comfortable chair. "Cornucopia's been looking after the babies all this time —"

"Never you mind," June-bug said, and pressed her right back down onto the worn calico cushion. "Word's been sent to Cornucopia — Toby went right away. As for the babies, why, little Emma Hargreaves has been helping her tend them, and she knows what she's doin', too, what with those little'uns of Trey and Rachel's."

Jessica settled back with a sigh and accepted another cup of June-bug's wonderful medicinal concoction. Her eyelids felt heavy, and it seemed that every muscle in her body had gone limp all of a sudden. She realized she couldn't have walked even as far as the newspaper office; she was simply too tired.

She drifted off after that, and someone carried her to a bed — a blessedly soft, warm, clean bed. She was vaguely aware of Dr. Parrish leaning over her, his stethoscope dangling from around his neck.

"Am I sick?" she asked, unsure even as

she uttered the words whether she was speaking aloud or simply thinking the question.

He smiled. "Just tired," he said. He sounded real, but he could be part of a dream.

Perhaps she was still in that freezing cabin after all, perhaps this delicious comfort, this cosseting warmth, was really a prelude to death. She'd read that it happened just this way. "Gage?"

"He's all right, too," Dr. Parrish assured her. "Get some rest."

She slipped beneath the surface of consciousness then, unable to stay afloat any longer, even if that meant she would never awaken.

When she opened her eyes again, the room was full of light, dazzling, snow-bounced light. And Gage was sitting on the edge of her narrow bed, grinning down at her. She blinked.

"I never thought I'd end up with a lazy wife," he said.

She blinked again. "Wife?"

"Jacob's agreed to marry us today," he went on, still smiling. "If you're still willing."

A great, jubilant shout of joy swelled within her, but she managed to contain it, and sat bolt upright instead. "What about the newspaper? The babies?"

He laughed. "We've talked about the newspaper and the babies, remember? We'll adopt the twins, and you can run the *Gazette* as long as it suits you. Just print a few favorable articles about the mayor now and then, if you don't mind."

Her mind was racing, but even at top speed, it couldn't catch up with her runaway heart. "But there's so much we don't know about each other, you and I —"

He kissed her forehead. "We've got a lifetime to learn," he replied. "What's your answer, Jessie? Yes or no?"

She stared at him for a long while. "Yes," she said finally. As if there had ever been any doubt, from the first moment she'd laid eyes on him.

Jacob performed the ceremony that afternoon, in the little white church with the bell tower, and despite the deep, hard-crusted snow that stretched, glittering, for miles in every direction, the pews were packed with delighted guests. June-bug sang a wedding song of her own composition, high and sweet, and the women wept with joy throughout the whole service.

Trey and Rachel Hargreaves served cake

and coffee in their decorous parlor when the ceremony was over, and at twilight, when the bride and groom finally took their leave, fat flakes of snow were swirling lazily down from a gray and low-bellied sky.

When Gage swept Jessica up in his arms, right there at the Hargreaves's front gate, a rousing cheer was raised by the wedding guests, gathered shivering on the porch to wave and call out good wishes. He looked down at her and frowned thoughtfully.

"What's the matter?" Jessica asked, still a little afraid he might change his mind about marriage. About her.

"You don't mind, do you? That I sold the house, I mean? I'd rather have one we planned together, but —"

Jessica thought her heart would burst; the love she felt for this man was so strong that it brought tears to her eyes and caused her breath to catch. "No," she said, because she was too stricken with happiness to embellish her words. "I don't mind. I just want to be with you."

He kissed her, right there in the middle of the street.

Cornucopia had taken the babies to the store before the wedding, and the tiny apartment over the newspaper office was empty. A note left on the kitchen table said they weren't to worry; the twins were being properly spoiled.

"That woman in San Francisco," she said, "do you still care for her?" It was the first time she'd dared ask, even though the possibility had been pulsing in her mind ever since Cornucopia had told her what she knew of Gage's past. While she'd related the whole story of her experience with Mr. Covington while they were stranded in the cabin, he had said little or nothing about his own past.

He smiled, still holding her. Her skirt trailed on the floor, and her hair, like his, was full of snow. He sat down, without releasing her, in the rocking chair facing the empty fireplace. "No," he said. "That's been over for a long time, Jessie. Besides, she's married to my brother."

She searched his face. "But you're estranged from them, aren't you? Your grandfather, your half-brother?"

He sighed. "Small towns," he said.

She flicked at a stray lock of his dark hair with the backs of her fingers. "Make things right with them, Gage," she urged softly. "Whatever happened, they're your family."

"You're my family," he said, kissing those same fingers. "You and the twins."

"You know what I mean," she insisted.

Once again, he sighed. "All right," he said. "I'll write to them. Extend the olive branch. But if they don't respond, there isn't much I can do about it."

She smiled, pleased. "What happened?"

"Could we talk about this later?" he was fiddling with her hair, watching her mouth as though it fascinated him.

"No," she replied.

He tilted his head back and closed his eyes. When he spoke, he seemed to be addressing the ceiling. "My grandfather told me that my father was dead, and I believed him. Hell, why wouldn't I? My mother remarried, had Luke. Then I found out that he'd lied — they all had. My grandfather had forced my father — his own son — out of the business, out of all our lives. Luke knew the truth, and he never told me. By the time I found out, it was too late."

"Your father really had died by that time?"

He nodded.

"And the woman?"

"She married Luke — my half-brother. As far as I know, they've been happy together."

Jessica was silent a long time. Then she laid her face against his cheek. "I'm sorry," she said.

He hooked a finger under her chin and

made her look at him. "Can we start the honeymoon now?"

She blushed, then nodded, and he carried her toward the bedroom and the bed where she had expected to sleep alone for the rest of her natural life.

"It's not a very fancy place to spend a wedding night," she observed, a little ruefully. They were at the threshold of their room now, moving inexorably toward a fate that made Jessica's breath catch. He paused, looked into her eyes.

"It'll do just fine," he said. "Springwater's changed me, Jessie. I'm not the same man I was when I came here." He laid her gently on the bed and began to undress her, starting by unlacing her shoes and tugging them off. He caressed her ankles for a while, all the while talking in a low, melodious voice, describing the things he wanted to make her feel in minute detail. Finally, he unfastened her garters, rolled down her stockings, stroked her bare legs.

Jessica felt as though she were coming down with a fever. Tendrils of her hair were already clinging to her temples and her nape, and she couldn't seem to get her breath. The sweet, cold silence of the snow falling outside did nothing to cool her blood.

She watched, unable to speak, as he shed his coat, undid his string tie, worked the buttons of his fine white shirt. A tantalizing view of his chest greeted her eyes; she tried not to stare and could not help herself. He was more than handsome, more than magnificent, and he was hers.

"Jessie," he said, his voice hoarse. They were both bare of every garment and constraint, lying face to face beneath the fine quilt that had simply been there when the coverlet was drawn back. "You trust me, don't you? Never to hurt you, I mean?"

She swallowed and nodded. After what they'd been through together, she would have trusted him with her soul as well as her body.

He ran a hand down her shoulder and arm, brought it to rest on her hip, and left a trail of small, invisible sparks arching off her flesh. "I'll be as gentle as I can," he promised, "but sometimes — just the first time — if you want me to stop —"

She laid an index finger to his mouth. "I want you to *start*, Gage. And don't stop until I'm yours and you're mine."

He kissed her again then, gently at first, then with growing hunger. It was quite different, that kiss, from its predecessors — lying naked together in their marriage bed changed everything.

Over the long, languorous interlude to follow, Gage introduced Jessica to a variety of simple but soul-searing pleasures, exploring the planes and curves and hollows of her body, her spirit, and her mind, and sharing those same parts of himself. Long before they actually joined themselves together physically, they had formed a mystical bond that even death could not sever.

At long last, Gage raised himself over her — she was pleading by then, half delirious with wanting — and he looked into her eyes with such tenderness that she was sure her heart must have cracked within her like an eggshell, made forever strong by its weakness.

"Say yes, Jessie," he said. "Please, say yes."

She couldn't get a word past her constricted throat, so she merely nodded again, and he was inside her, in a long, unbroken stroke, filling her, exalting her, setting her ablaze. There was a suggestion of pain, but that was soon lost in a maelstrom of rising need; they flung themselves together, apart, together, faster and faster.

Then, in the space of a heartbeat, the universe splintered into glittering pieces, licked with flame, and showered down around them, bits of shattered sky, stars, and memories of stars. They were everything and nothing at all. They were themselves, and each other, and wholly separate. But some part of them, Jessica knew, even in those breathless moments when she was sure she could not survive such ecstasy, would always be one being, always live at the heights.

As they slept entwined, snowflakes pirouetted past the windows and blanketed the earth in a mantle of glorious white.

June of 1998
Port Orchard

Dear Friends,

Welcome to the Springwater stagecoach station, which will grow over the next few months, before your very eyes, into a thriving community, complete with a saloon, a schoolhouse, a church, and a newspaper, among other things. There are six books in the Springwater series, although I may do more. I love the idea of writing a long, involved story and watching this fictional town full of delightful people come to life. I hope the many and varied characters will become as dear to you as they are to me.

Let me know what you think, and to receive a copy of the *Springwater Gazette*, Springwater's own newspaper, please send a business-sized stamped, self-addressed envelope, with your address clearly printed. We'll add you to the newsletter list automatically, thus giving you advance notice of every new release, whether it is part of this series or separate. The address is:

Linda Lael Miller
P.O. Box 669
Port Orchard, WA 98366
e-mail: lindalaelm@aol.com

God bless and keep.

Warmly,

Linda Lael Miller

The employees of Thorndike Press hope you have enjoyed this Large Print book. All our Large Print titles are designed for easy reading, and all our books are made to last. Other Thorndike Press Large Print books are available at your library, through selected bookstores, or directly from us.

For information about titles, please call:

(800) 257-5157

To share your comments, please write:

Publisher
Thorndike Press
P.O. Box 159
Thorndike, Maine 04986